A Nov

THE GRAY
BROTHERS
WEDDING

JOHANNA DELACRUZ

CHAPTER 1

WHAT THE HELL WAS THAT?

I stood there, looking at Nash as he was on bended knee. Then I did what any normal, sane girl would do. I ran away.

"What the hell?" Nash asked.

"Uh, Nash, that shouldn't have happened," Noah said.

"Thank you, Captain Obvious," Nixon said.

Nash stood up and looked at them.

"What are you waiting for, Nash? Go after her, you tool!" They told him.

"Oh, right," he said as he chased after me.

They shook their heads while rolling their eyes.

"This wedding will be interesting," Nate said as everyone gave him a skeptical look.

"Mags! Stop!" I heard him say as he ran after me until he tackled me.

Well, damn it.

He flipped me over and sat on top of me. "A simple yes or no would have sufficed."

"Sorry, I panicked." I gave him a sheepish look.

"You panicked?" He gave me a strange look as I gave him an innocent smile.

"Yep." I nodded my head.

"You ran."

"Yep."

"Really?"

"Well, everyone was looking at me, and they made me nervous."

"This situation seems familiar," Pat said to Nate as they walked up.

Nate rolled his eyes. "You won't let that go, will you?"

"You made me drop my Slurpee."

"I replaced said Slurpee."

We watched Nate and Pat as they bickered over a Slurpee. I'll never understand why.

Nash shook his head. "Well?"

"Yes." Then I smiled as he crashed his lips into mine.

"Well, it's about damn time! Can we eat now?" We heard Nixon ask. Oh, boy. Never get between Nixon and food when he wants to eat. It never ends well.

Nash got off me and helped me up. He slid the engagement ring onto my left ring finger. Then he slipped his hand into mine, leading me back towards the restaurant.

We took our seats as Nate stood up and tapped his glass, getting everyone's attention.

"I would like everyone's attention!" He said as we looked at him.

"Of course," Nixon said, making everyone snicker.

"My son, the comedian." He shot Nixon a look, who put his hands up in defense. "I watched this young woman grow up and become the wonderful lady she is today. It took a lot to get to this point, but we did. I'm so happy to have her become a part of our family. To Maggie!" He toasted me.

"Hey, what about me?" Nash asked Nate.

"Yeah, you, too."

We laughed.

"Thanks, Dad!" Nash said.

"Well, you have been a tool. We need some good in this family," Pat said.

"Ma!" Nash said.

"Do I lie? No. Now, hush, you tool."

Nash grumbled as I giggled. Poor Nash. He couldn't catch a break no matter what he did. I leaned over and kissed his cheek.

They brought dinner to us. While we ate, we talked.

"So, are you ready, Maggie?" Nathan asked me.

"Ready to get married? Definitely," I said.

"No. Nathan means are you ready for the wedding planning?" Noah asked.

"Huh?" I asked.

"Oh, Margaret. I'm glad I caught you before you took off like a banshee. I have so many ideas for your wedding," Lucille said as she walked over to me.

I looked at everyone as they became quiet. Oh, boy. Why will the wedding planning get crazy?

*****

After fending off Lucille, thanks to Pat, everyone had left. Nash and I stayed since the restaurant was on the beach. We took off our shoes and walked around barefoot.

Feeling the sand flow through my toes always reminded me of the summer days. I loved the feeling. Nash held my hand as we walked.

"You know, for a minute, I thought you would have said no," he said.

"And what if I did?"

He stopped and turned to me. "I was praying you didn't."

Nash held a serious gaze.

"Nash?"

"Mags." He dropped his shoes and took my hands into his. "I lost you a few times. I couldn't bear to lose you again. I lost a part of me when I lost you. You make me whole. Without you, I'm empty. With you, I'm alive."

A smile curled upon my lips. "It doesn't matter. I would have said yes."

He placed his hand under my chin as he pulled me into a kiss. He gave me a sweet kiss until he deepened it. I put my hands on his back as I kissed him back.

Today marked a turning point for us. We were on our way to start our lives together forever. First, we needed to deal with Lucille and the rest of the Grays. What could go wrong?

CHAPTER 2

IT SEEMS LIKE OLD TIMES

After getting engaged, we had to deal with questions about wedding planning. I told everyone they could do whatever they wanted. I wanted to get through my senior year of college. Nash thought I was crazy. Considering I'm marrying into his family, he was right.

Before I knew it, the summer flew by. We returned to school for our senior year. Now we had Nolan and his girlfriend Brook with us. The last girl he met didn't last. It's an excellent thing that I couldn't remember her.

We made our way back to school. It took about three hours to arrive. I found out we were in a new house with the brothers, the girls, and me. The cousins had their own rental home, along with our roommates having their own.

College life would get crazy.

We got out of the car and grabbed items to take inside. Nash opened the door, and we stopped dead in our tracks.

"Nix, I thought you found a nice place?" Nash asked Nixon.

"I was busy, so I told Nathan to do it," Nixon said.

"And I told Noah to find something," Nathan said.

"But then I asked Nolan to do it," Noah said.

"What's wrong with the place? It has character," Nolan said as we looked at him like he had lost his mind.

"Dude, it's a freaking dump, like your head," Nixon said.

"Oh, come on. When Ma and Dad moved into their house, it wasn't the best, but they fixed it up," he said.

"Because they had help and were planning on living there the rest of their lives, you tool!" Nixon said.

As Nixon and Nolan bickered, I walked in and set a box down, looking around. It wasn't a terrible house, but it needed work.

"Mags?" I heard Nash's voice.

I turned and looked at everyone as they stared at me.

"I've got an idea," I said.

The brothers looked at each other, then back at me.

*****

"You want to fix this dump up?" Carson asked us.

"Yep," I said.

"Have you lost your mind?" Caleb asked me as everyone looked at him.

"Nope, only my memory." I grinned.

"Nope. I'm sure you lost your mind," Cody said.

"Okay." I shrugged as they smirked, then I pulled out my phone and dialed a number.

"Wait. Who are you calling?" Carson asked me.

"Why do you care? Now, hush." I waved him off as the line connected. "Hey, it's me. Yeah, we have arrived, but there's a slight issue. Well, the boys passed the buck. Now we are moving into a rundown house. Yep, I'm sure. You will! That's great! I'll tell them! Okay, see you soon." I smiled as I hung up the phone.

"Maggie, who did you call?" Jace asked me as I smiled.

"I called someone who would see things my way." I shrugged.

"Who?" They asked.

I gave them an innocent smile.

✸✸✸✸✸

A few hours later, there was a knock on the door as it fell inward onto the floor. Grayson, Nate, Jonas, and Cayson stood there as Nate held his hand up from knocking.

"You called our dads," Jaime said.

"No," I said.

"You called Grandpa," Noah said.

"Nope," I said.

"Huh?" They asked.

"I called Lucille," I spoke with enthusiasm while grinning.

They looked at me like I lost my mind as I smiled. Then I heard someone say, "Well, don't stand there like statues. We have much work to do."

"Who's this we?" Nate asked as Lucille walked inside.

She smiled a devilish smile as everyone groaned.

I learned one thing while living with the Grays and getting to know everyone again. If you want to execute a crazy idea, you need to go to the source themselves. It's none other than Lucille. She might be crazy, but at least, she gets things done.

Plus, I might have mentioned that Nash and I were eloping if we didn't get help. That didn't sit well with her. Pat even admitted I was learning well and had great potential in this family. God, I hope so.

*****

We got to work. With each of us helping, it wouldn't take long to repair the place. With Lucille directing everyone, I'm sure they wanted to complete the repairs quickly.

We cleaned, painted, and fixed the plumbing and electrical. At one point, the lights went out, and someone said, "My bad!" Yeah, Jonas was doing the electrical repairs.

Nate said, "Your bad? I'm going to 'your bad' on your head!"

Damn, Nate has a temper.

"Uh, weren't you going to help, Dad?" Cody asked Cayson.

"Nope, they have everything under control," he said, fixing the door with Carson as we heard a crashing sound. We stopped as he said, "Then again, I guess not."

We ran to the basement to find Jonas rubbing his head and Nate steaming.

"I got this," Grayson said, separating them. I thought the boys were rough, but they had nothing on their father and uncles. It'll be a long week.

*****

Did you ever feel you're living in the Twilight Zone? I felt that way the entire week. Between the arguing and craziness with everyone, it was wearing on me. My head would throb. I tried to hide it, but that only made it worse.

The stress was getting to me, which the doctor had recommended that I keep low. Yeah, sure, doctor. Have you met the Grays?

At one point, the stress became too much, and everything started spinning.

"Uh, Maggie, you don't look so good," Nolan said.

I lost my coloring and my balance. As I fell, Nash caught me. "Mags?" I heard Nash say. Then everything went black.

"Nash?" Nate asked.

"I need someone to get me a cold compress and a glass of water," he said.

"What's going on, Nash?" Lucille asked, walking over to us.

"It's the stress. The doctor said stress would cause her to pass out. She needs to take it easy." He stroked my hair as he held me.

"Here," Nate said, handing him the items. He tried to rouse me. My eyes fluttered open, and I looked at everyone. Then I looked at Nash.

"It happened again, didn't it?" I asked him, sighing.

"Yeah," he said.

"I'm sorry."

"Mags, it's okay. You need to tell me if things are getting too much."

I sat up, taking the water as I took a sip. "I didn't want anyone to worry."

"I know, but you need to tell me."

I sighed. I didn't want everyone to worry about me. I put everyone through so much.

"Maggie, you're family. We worry about you no matter what," Nixon said to me.

"Okay." I sighed.

Nash wrapped his arms around me and held me close. I knew I made the right decision to say yes to Nash. With the Grays' craziness, they cared about me. For that, their concern made me grateful.

After that brief episode, they ordered me to stay with my brother. I don't know who was crazier, the Grays or my brother. It's still a toss-up.

Life was about to get crazier with everyone, including me.

CHAPTER 3

SETTLING IN

They completed the house repairs, albeit with a few minor mishaps. I don't even want to know what they were. I came home, Nash helped me settle, and then the fun started with Marco and Brook.

"So, you're Nolan's girl," he said, eyeing her.

"The last time I checked." She shrugged.

"And you have his best intentions at heart?"

"I would think so."

"What do you mean, you think so? You don't know?"

"Well, I would like to say I do. Then again, you never know."

"That is not an answer. The answer is yes or no."

"And who are you?" She pointed at him.

"Who am I? I am The Fabulous Marco! And I am outstanding!"

"Who says?" She looked at him like he was crazy.

"Well." He thought about it. "Everyone."

"Uh-huh, sure, you are," She rolled her eyes.

We came downstairs to see everyone watching them.

"I am. Who are you? Oh, that's right. I'm Brook. I'm the greatest thing since sliced bread. Pft, yeah, right."

"Oh, I'm Marco. I'm gay and fabulous. Love me."

"You mock, moi." He feigned shock.

"Pbbbt, yes, yes, I did. Only because you mocked me first."

"You, you, you hussy!"

"Well, you, you, you, no fashion sense, doof!"

"Ah! You offend me!"

I stood there and watched them. It was the stupidest fight I had ever seen. I walked over to Marco and Brook.

"Ladies, it's time to put your claws away," I told them.

"Humph." Marco pouted.

"Oh, for crying out loud! Stop being a drama queen, Marco," I said as Brook stuck her tongue out. Then I turned to Brook. "And you stop egging him on."

She rolled her eyes at me.

"I don't have time for both of your craps. So, knock it off," I said.

"But Maggie," he said, whining.

"Enough, Marco. You be good," I told him as he whimpered. "Now, Brook is a pleasant girl considering she's with Nolan. I would say that gives her points."

"Hey!" Nolan said.

I glanced at Nolan. "Is it my fault you're a panty thief?"

"Not panties, but bras," he said.

I rolled my eyes at him.

"You're not helping your cause, little man," Nash told him.

"I'm not little," Nolan said, crossing his arms.

"Yeah, sure you aren't," Nixon said.

"No, he isn't. He's well endowed," Brook said, causing Nolan to smirk.

"I don't need to hear about my brother's dick size," Nathan said.

"Only because you're smaller than the rest," Noah said.

"I am not!"

"Bro, I shared a room with you for years. Yes, you are."

"You should talk. I'm sure my pinky is bigger than you, even when you're hard."

Then the shit hit the fan. Why do guys always argue about the size of their manhood?

Nash leaned over and said in a low voice, "I hope I'm not small."

I did a double-take and said, "Far from it." That made him smile. Great, now my fiancé was self-conscious about his manhood. Where did I go wrong?

The door opened, and in walked Jasper and Paul. This day gets better and better.

"What is going on here?" Jasper asked us.

"Well, the boys are arguing about their dick size," Kat said as the other girls stood there, watching.

"Well, uh, okay," he said, confused.

"But it started with Marco and Brook," Marcy said.

"How did Marco and a girl's argument lead into arguing about dick size?" Paul asked them.

"Because they're the Gray brothers. They argue over everything, duh," Macey said while rolling her eyes.

"Huh?" Paul asked.

"What my sister means," Marcy said, giving Macey a look. "With the Gray brothers, anything is fair game, including someone's manhood, including if they have blue balls."

"Yep," Macey said.

"Blue balls?" He cocked his head at them.

"If a brother doesn't get any and can't shoot his load, he develops blue balls," Marcy said.

"I know what blue balls are. I'm a guy, for Christ's sake," Paul said.

"When someone gets blue balls, they have a cake to mourn said blue balls," Marcy said.

"A cake?" He arched an eyebrow at her.

"It's like a tradition, plus the Grays love their cake," Kat said.

"This family is strange," he said, waving his pointer finger.

"You have no idea," Marcy said.

After listening to everyone argue for what seemed like hours. It's only been thirty minutes. I said, "Enough!"

They stopped at once.

"I've had it with the bickering. Who cares who is more endowed?" I looked at the twins. "Who cares who is dating who?" I looked at Marco. "This conversation is ridiculous, and you know it."

They looked at me.

"Now, can we stop arguing and try to get along?"

Everyone went back to bickering. I threw my hands up into the air. "I give up." I went upstairs. Life with the Grays has been an adventure. It would become even bigger.

*****

I laid on the bed with my face shoved into a pillow. Then someone sat on my butt. I didn't even need to ask who it was.

Hands pressed on my back, massaging it. It felt nice. I hadn't realized how tense my body was with everything. Ever since we got engaged, issues had magnified ten times more than they were.

"Mags, are you okay?" His voice was soft and deep, calming me.

"Yeah." I sighed. "Ever since we got engaged, things have gotten more chaotic."

He climbed off me, lying next to me. I turned my head and looked at him.

"You're not changing your mind, are you?" He asked me.

"What? No."

"Good, because I don't want to deal with Grammy or my ma." He sighed.

"Nash, I love you, and I can't wait to marry you. Sometimes, things can get too much."

"Tell me about it." He turned onto his side and faced me while stroking my arm with his finger. "I want you to know that marrying you makes me happy. Everything we have been through makes it worthwhile."

I couldn't help but smile.

"Baby girl, I love it when you smile, knowing I'm causing your smile and not your tears."

Nash looked pained. I knew he had felt guilty for things that had happened, but he shouldn't. Everyone makes mistakes.

I placed my hand on his cheek and leaned in as I kissed him. I wanted to reassure him I was fine and we were okay. He got the hint when he pulled me to him, deepening the kiss. It was so tender until banging against the wall interrupted us. Ugh.

We stopped and looked at each other.

"It sounds like Nolan and Beth broke in their room." He smirked. I placed my palm on my face.

Oh, hell, no. I wouldn't listen to that all night long. I got up, storming over to the door.

"Mags! Where are you going?"

"To tell Mr. Horn dog to keep it down!"

Nash ran after me. I stormed over to Nolan's door and banged on it. "Nolan! No one wants to hear you banging your girlfriend!"

Another door opened. Nolan and Brook stuck their heads out. "What are you complaining about now? We aren't even doing anything!" Nolan told me.

"Wait. Isn't this your room?" I pointed at the door.

"Does it look like my room? No."

"Then whose room is it?"

The door opened, and I got smacked with a pillow. "It's my room, you dink."

I stood face to face with Nathan as he glared at me. "Do you mind? Macey and I were busy. Now go away." He slammed the door in my face.

I stood there, horrified. Oh, God.

"Mags?"

I didn't say a word as I hurried past Nash and down the stairs. I walked out of the front door after becoming mortified. I needed to get out of there, so I ran. I heard Nash yelling, but I didn't stop. I kept running.

I needed to breathe. Breathe, Maggie, breathe.

CHAPTER 4

BREATH, JUST BREATHE

I ran until I reached Marco's house, then pounded on his door. He opened it, looking bewildered by my presence until I clung to him.

"Maggie?" He asked as I clung to him.

"Marco, oh, God." I gasped. I couldn't even form sentences. The walls were closing in on me, and the room was spinning. My stress level was through the roof.

"Jasper! Help!"

Jasper came running downstairs and found me in a state. "She's having a panic attack. Hold on to her while I get my bag." He took off to his room while I grasped Marco's shirt.

Nash found us. "Mags!"

"Nash, make it stop!" I started hyperventilating. Jasper returned and injected me with something. Everything went black.

*****

After a few minutes, my eyelids fluttered open. I saw a bunch of faces staring at me, startling me. "Ah!"

Nash grabbed me. "It's okay, Mags."

I calmed down and took a deep breath. Then I fell backward onto the couch.

"Well, at least, she isn't dead," Nixon said, causing everyone to look at him. "What? You try to explain to Ma why Nathan killed Maggie."

"I didn't kill her," Nathan said.

"Not on purpose," Noah said.

"She shouldn't have been pounding on my door like a raging lunatic," he said.

Nash stood up and looked at his brother. "Shut up."

Nathan looked at him.

"I'm tired of your attitude. You act like an ass, and enough is enough."

"Nash, that's not fair," Nathan told him.

"No. What's not fair is you can't handle your damn insecurity. You must be nasty to people. Nix isn't as nasty as you are. Grow up." Nash turned, leaning over as he helped me up.

He walked me to the door as Nathan said, "Oh, I'm sorry. We're not as perfect as you!"

Nash stopped and was about to charge Nathan when I stopped him. "Stop." Nash looked at me as I held his arm. "Please, Nash. Don't do this."

He sighed. "Okay, Mags. Let's get you home."

I nodded, and he helped me home.

Nixon looked at Nathan. "Dude, Maggie saved your ass. It would help if you got your temper under control. You know damn well that Nash has Dad's temper." He walked away.

I didn't want the boys to fight. I don't know what happened because it was a new development and scared the hell out of me.

Once we got home, the girls met us at the door. I had worried about them as much as everyone else. I wanted to go to bed. The episode had exhausted me.

Nash helped me upstairs, and I got ready for bed. I sat down and sighed.

"Mags?"

"Nash, I'm scared. I haven't felt this way since the last time."

He crouched in front of me. "Okay, tomorrow, we'll go see the doctor."

I nodded. I didn't want to get sick again since it was scary the first time. I didn't want to go through it again.

*****

The next day Nash took me to the doctors. The doctor did a complete examination of me. He figured out what was happening to me. I was having issues with my blood pressure. The more stress I was under, the more my blood pressure would rise.

My blood pressure caused a panic attack. It was my body's way of compensating. He prescribed me medication to help and ordered me to reduce my stress. Ha! That is easier said than done.

We left the doctor's office, and I became defeated once again.

"Mags." Nash stopped me. "Look, I know you feel down, but we'll get through this together." He pulled me into a hug.

"Nash, I'm tired of something always being wrong with me. I feel useless," I said into his chest.

"I know, baby girl. I know. We're in it for the long haul. I promise."

He reassured me to a point, but we still had to deal with the wedding.

"What?" He asked.

"Oh, it's nothing. We have to get through our senior year along with planning a wedding."

"I have an idea."

What did he have planned?

*****

"Are you freaking kidding me? Ma will kill you if you do this," Nixon said.

"That's why we won't say anything to anyone," Nash said.

"Okay, but Grammy will kill you," Noah said.

"Not if you guys keep your trap shut."

The boys looked at each other. I sat there, listening. How the hell do we get around this without someone spilling their guts? I mean, if it's one thing the Gray boys do well, they throw each other under the bus.

"Look, we do this with quietness, then let them have their day. Then Maggie can relax and not stress," Nash said.

"You know the minute someone finds out, and word gets back to them, our asses are in a sling," Nathan said.

"Who will talk?" Nash asked them.

"Did you forget about our loving family who likes nothing more than to sink us?" Nolan said.

"That's an appropriate point. We'll make sure our family doesn't find out," Nash said.

As they conspired, I sat there and thought about it. Then it hit me. Nash and I wanted to get married, but the day wasn't about us. It was a chance for people to celebrate with us. Even with the family's craziness, I couldn't take away Pat's chance to see her firstborn get married. It wouldn't be fair to her.

"No," I said.

They stopped and looked at me.

"What?" Nash asked.

I stood up and placed my hands on his hands. "We can't do this. Yeah, it's less stressful. But Nash, your family, has done so much for me. I can't take this one thing from them and lie about it."

"Are you sure about this?"

"I'm positive. Look, yes, it's stressful. Yes, Nathan can be an ass." I looked at Nathan as he rolled his eyes. "But your mom means the world to me. I can't take away her chance to watch her firstborn marry." I looked at them. "When each of you gets married, Pat's there to hand you off to your wife. With each wedding, things become sadder for her. She knows you will start a life with someone else."

"Have you met our ma?" Nixon asked me.

"Yes. What does that have to do with anything?"

"Maggie, no offense. Ma is waiting to unload us on a poor unsuspecting girl. That way, she doesn't have to deal with us and our shenanigans," Noah said.

How is it that I try to make a beautiful speech, and they kill it with reality? Oh, that's right. They're the Gray brothers.

"I say you guys do it. Get it over with now. We'll have the wedding later," Nolan said, agreeing with Nash.

Nash looked at me as I looked at him. Do we want to do this?

*****

The answer is yes, as we stood outside of City Hall. I took a deep breath as we walked inside. The brothers and I would do the unthinkable. Did we go through with it?

CHAPTER 5

HERE WE GO AGAIN

We left City Hall and didn't speak one word to each other. Cooler heads prevailed on this one. Sometimes, I had to wonder what the boys were thinking.

We went to school to get our schedules and books. I wanted to put this idea far away from me. All I wanted to do was focus on our senior year and the wedding, even with Lucille involved with it. Oh, boy.

Once we arrived, we got our schedules along with our books. We ran into the demon spawn themselves. I talked to the girls while the boys talked to their cousins until Caleb spotted a girl talking to two other girls.

"Now that's what I'm talking about." He smirked.

"Who?" Cody asked him.

"Her." Caleb pointed at a redhead.

"Dude, no way," Cody said.

"Yes, and she's fucking hot." He rubbed his hands together.

I knew the girls they were discussing. Meg was the redhead, Gema was the one with black hair, and Becca was the brunette. Caleb was talking about Meg and good luck. Meg has lofty standards. Caleb, well, he wasn't high enough.

"Dude, I'm telling you. If you go over there, you'll trip and fall flat on your face," Cody told him.

"Ye has little faith," he said as he started walking over to the three girls.

"I hope you enjoy eating dirt, you tool!" Cody told him.

"Bite me!" Caleb said.

"What's that idiot doing now?" Carson asked us as he walked up to us. He watched his brother walk towards the three girls.

"He's about to get his ass handed to him by one of the hottest girls here," Cody said.

"Good. You would think Caleb would have learned from Maggie hitting him. Maggie, do you think you could hit him again to knock some sense into his stupid ass?" He asked me. Nash and I looked at Carson, who shrugged. "It's a suggestion."

We watched Caleb approach Meg.

"Well, hello, there," he said, trying to act smooth. The operative word would be smooth.

"Can I help you?" She arched an eyebrow.

"Yeah. You, I, and a date." Caleb smirked.

"And what makes you think I would go on a date with you?"

"Because sweetheart, I am the guy of your dreams."

"Who says?"

"Says me."

"Doubt it." She rolled her eyes.

"Look, lady. You should feel privileged to have a Gray hitting on you."

"And that's our cue before she rips off his balls," Cody said as he and Carson walked over to Caleb.

"Ladies! Sorry about our dipshit brother," Cody told them. "He has no manners."

"Of course," Meg said.

"We apologize for his lewd behavior," Cody said.

"Speak for yourself," Carson told him.

"Carson, you're not helping," Cody said.

"Don't care." He shrugged.

"Well, you're charming," Meg told Carson.

"I don't do charming or anything else. I don't do girls who think they're all that. I don't care."

"Well, you're a sweet guy."

"I am not sweet, sweetheart. You couldn't handle someone like me."

"Oh, I know I can." She smirked.

He looked her up and down. "Yeah, I don't think so." With that, he walked away.

"Wait. Did Carson blow me off?" She asked, looking at her friends.

"Girl, he blew you like the wind." Gema snickered as she gestured back and forth with her hand.

"Oh, hell, no!" She ran after Carson.

"So, what's your name?" Becca asked Cody.

"Who?" He asked her.

"You."

"Cody."

"Well, Cody, how do you feel about Harry Potter?"

"I like Harry Potter." He shrugged.

"Great!" She grabbed his hand while dragging him off.

Caleb watched as they chased both his brothers and stood there with the last girl. He furrowed his brows.

"For what it's worth, I find an assertive man, hot." He heard someone say with a giggle.

He turned and raised his brows. "Oh, you do, do you?"

"Yep." She nodded.

"Well, in that case, let me show you how assertive I am." He wrapped his arm around the girl's shoulder, leading her away.

I watched as three boys ended up with three girls. Well, except Carson, who blew off Meg. That situation should be interesting.

"And there goes the Gray charm." Nolan smirked.

We looked at him as he shrugged. It would be an exciting combination with those three.

Everyone splits up. Nash and I walked around campus, talking about our classes when someone walked up to us.

"Hey, Maggie," Meg said.

"Hey, Meg," I said.

She looked at Nash. "You're Nash Gray, aren't you?"

"Last time I checked," he said.

"Oh, well, I need your help," she said while dragging Nash away.

I shrugged, then walked away. I went back to the house to take a nap. Today has been an eventful day. I saw Nathan and Macey in the living room when I returned.

"Where's Nash?" Nathan asked me.

"He's off with Meg somewhere." I shrugged.

"What?"

"I'm too tired to worry about it. I'm going to lie down." I yawned as I made my way upstairs.

"We'll check on you in a few, Maggie," Macey said as I nodded.

They heard the door close a few minutes later. "I swear I'll kick Nash's ass if he goes back to the way things were before," Nathan said.

"Relax, I don't think Nash would do that."

"Are you sure? My brother can be a tool, especially with Maggie. Everything he had put her through was ridiculous. I'm glad she doesn't remember it."

"Nathan."

"Macey, Maggie and I have our differences. She deserves better than someone on the fence about her."

"Yeah, but I don't think Nash is on the fence anymore. I'll be the first person who would kick his ass if he hurt her again. We should get our facts before jumping to conclusions."

"When did you become reasonable?"

"When I started dating a Gray brother." She smirked, causing Nathan to roll his eyes.

A few minutes later, Nixon walked in with Kat. "Get a room," he said while plopping down in a chair, then pulled Kat onto his lap.

"Whatever," Nathan said as he rolled his eyes. "Did you hear our dipshit brother is back at it again?"

"What are you talking about?"

"Well, Maggie is upstairs alone taking a nap, and Nash is off with Meg somewhere."

"There's no way. Nash would be a huge tool if he pulled his shit again."

"Well, actions speak louder than words, brother."

Nixon looked at him as the other four walked in.

"What's up with frick and frack?" Noah asked, pointing to Nathan and Nixon.

"Well, they think your brother is messing around on Maggie. Or it's something like that," Macey said.

"No way," Noah said.

"So, explain why Maggie is upstairs sleeping alone, and Nash is with Meg?" Nathan asked him.

"Well, uh, shit," Noah said while rubbing the back of his neck.

"Exactly," Nathan said with a look.

"That's ridiculous," Marcy said.

"Is it?" Nixon asked her.

"Well… never mind." She sighed.

They sat there, contemplating how they would confront their big brother.

"Should I buy everyone a trampoline?" Brook asked

"Huh?" They asked.

"Well, you're jumping to conclusions. You don't even know if what you're saying is true. You're reacting to Maggie here without Nash."

"Well, how the hell should we take it?" Nixon asked her.

"There's more to it than what you think. I'm saying that you need to relax and talk to Nash before accusing him of something he isn't doing." She earned glares from the brothers. "Tough room."

The brothers heard the door handle turn as they got to their feet. As the door opened, they pounced on Nash. Yep, things were about to get ugly.

CHAPTER 6

THINGS ARE ABOUT TO GET UGLY AND SO, ARE YOU

I awoke to a commotion coming from downstairs. What in the world was going on? I rubbed my eyes and got up. I opened the door, making my way downstairs. I saw the brothers on top of Nash. What in the hell was going on?

I walked downstairs until I stood in front of them with my arms crossed.

"Uh, guys," Marcy said, trying to get their attention.

"Not now, Marcy," Noah said.

"Guys," Kat said.

"Kat, not now," Nixon said.

"Hey, losers!" Macey said.

They stopped, turning to see me standing there with my arms crossed and an unamused look on my face.

"Oh," said Nolan.

They stood up and backed away from Nash. He got up and wiped the blood from his mouth.

"Would someone explain to me why my fiancé's idiot brothers are beating him up?" I asked them.

"They think," Brook said, pointing at everyone, "Nash is cheating on you with Meg. It's because of past issues you guys had."

"What?" Nash and I both said.

"Well, you said Nash left with Meg," Nathan said.

"Because she dragged him off," I said.

"And it's not like Nash has the best history where it concerns you with other women," Noah said.

"Good point," Nixon said.

"So, what will you do about it, Maggie? I say you should kick his ass!" Nolan said.

The others nodded.

I narrowed my eyes and cocked my head. "No!"

"No?" They asked.

"I said no. First, did you bother to ask Nash what happened?" I asked them.

"Well, no," Nixon said.

"Exactly. Look, I get you that guys worry. It's sweet but creepy. Nash made a promise to me. I have to trust him," I said, defending Nash. I glanced at Nash. "You didn't, did you?"

He rolled his eyes. "No."

I shrugged. "See, there you have it."

"Okay. What was Nash doing with Meg?" Nixon asked while turning to Nash, which made us look at him.

"What happened?" I asked Nash.

"Meg wanted to know more about Carson." Nash shrugged.

"Carson!" They spoke.

"Yes, Carson. Our cousin blew her off. She wanted to know how to get him not to blow her off," he said.

"And what did you tell her?" Nixon asked him.

"I told her that he's Carson. He doesn't like anyone except her," he said, pointing at me, causing everyone to look at me. I placed my palm on my face.

Then we heard someone say, "Is this a terrible time?"

We turned to see Meg standing there.

*****

I had the chore of talking to Carson. Meg was upstairs with the girls. It's not what I meant by focusing on my senior year. I meant school, not other people.

Carson walked in. "Hey, Maggie. What's going on?"

"Carson, can we talk?"

He looked at me, and I gave him an innocent smile. It took time, but I talked to him about Meg. He was less than enthused.

"I'm not interested." He shrugged.

"Why not?"

"Because I'm not."

"What do you mean you're not interested?" We heard a voice asked as we turned to see Meg coming downstairs. He stood up and looked at me as I looked around.

Then he turned to her. "Because I'm not. You're hot, but it doesn't mean shit."

"Well, your tattoos mean nothing," she said.

"Wait. How do you know I have tats?"

"No reason." She walked past him and through the doorway. He looked at me, and I shrugged. Then Nash walked in. Well, shit, this wasn't good.

He glared at Nash and a clenched jaw. "I'll kill you."

"What did I do?" Nash asked.

Everything became complicated.

*****

"You know, I didn't plan on having to break up another fight tonight," I said, dabbing Nash's eyebrow with peroxide.

"Yeah, well, how fair is it I have to deal not only with my brothers but my cousin? It was much easier to take him when he was smaller." Nash sighed, making me giggle.

"Oh, you think that is funny," he said, pulling me to him while he started tickling me. I roared with laughter.

While Nash was busy with me, Carson found Meg.

*****

"Hey!" He said, getting Meg's attention.

She stopped and turned to him as he walked over to her. Her eyes widened.

"Let's get one thing straight. I don't like you," Carson told Meg.

Before she said anything, he pulled her into a kiss. Things got heated as they ended up in her dorm room. As things progressed, he stopped.

"Wait. Don't stop. It was getting juicy," Meg said while capturing Carson's lips with her own. He pulled away and left. She sat there, shocked.

He headed back to his house, making his way to his brothers' rooms and pounding on their doors. Both doors opened with a half-naked Cody and Caleb, along with Becca and Gema.

"Do you mind?" Caleb asked him.

"Are you serious?" Carson asked them.

"Dude, it's been a long time," Cody said.

"I don't care. Get dressed," Carson told his brothers. Then he walked away.

"How is it every time he has a chance to have sex, he ruins it for us?" Caleb asked Cody.

"You got me. It's Carson." He shrugged.

They threw on some clothes and came downstairs. Carson paced back and forth.

"Dude, what's the problem?" Cody asked him.

He stopped. "I kissed that chick."

"Who?" Caleb asked.

"That Meg chick," he said.

"Okay, and?" Caleb asked.

"And I don't like her," he said.

"Huh?" They asked.

"I mean, I like her, but I don't like her. Do you understand?"

"No, but you'll tell us," Caleb said.

"I've only liked one girl a lot," he said.

"Carson, she's getting married to our cousin," Cody said, taking a seat on the couch.

"It could change. You never know," Carson said.

"Bro, she is marrying our cousin. You remember him, don't you? Tall, dark hair, steel-grey eyes, has Uncle Nate's temper," Caleb said.

"Semantics," Carson said as he shrugged.

Caleb sat next to Cody.

"Look, I figure if I could get Maggie to see that we belong together, then it'll make her happy. I'm happy. Mr. Winky's happy," he said as he wiggled his eyebrows at them.

"Or be happy with someone else," a voice said. The triplets saw the other two girls coming downstairs.

"And what do you know?" He asked them.

"Well, for starters, you have a weird obsession with your cousin's chick," Gema said. "It's weird, but whatever. Next, Meg is hot. Is she not?"

"Oh, she's hot," Becca said.

"Get your head out of your ass and go after her," Gema told him.

"Who, Maggie?" He asked her.

"No, dumbshit, Meg." She rolled her eyes at him.

"But I don't like her."

"You're a dumbass, aren't you?"

"And you're a twit."

"You have such a lovely personality there, buddy. No wonder the girls are fawning over you." She smirked.

"Does this concern you? No. So, I don't want your opinion."

Caleb stood and said, "Okay, that's enough. Just because you're pissing and moaning over someone that you'll never get doesn't mean you can be a dick."

Then the demon spawn started arguing. Well, at least, Caleb and Carson fought while Cody made a call. Who did he call? It was none other than a brother. The only way to deal with a Gray is with a Gray.

*****

Bang! Bang! Bang!

Cody answered the door to find Nixon standing there.

"Aww, why did you have to call him?" Carson asked.

"Because unlike Nash, who is becoming soft, Nixon can still kick your ass," Cody said.

"That figures."

Nixon walked in, then looked at Carson and Caleb. "And here people thought I had anger issues." He scoffed.

"Nixon, will you tell dumbass here that he can't have Maggie. It's time for him to move on," Cody said, pointing to Carson.

Nixon looked at Carson. "It's time to move on, dumbass."

Carson gave him a look.

"What?" Nixon asked.

"But I love her," he said.

"No. You love that Maggie won't put up with your shit. Now pack a bag and move on."

Carson looked at him.

"Don't make me call your mother," Nixon told him.

"You wouldn't."

"Yeah, you're right, I wouldn't."

"Whew."

Knock, knock, knock.

The demon spawn looked at the door. Nixon answered it to find Dominique standing there.

"Nixon!" They spoke.

"So, I lied." He shrugged. "Sue me."

Dominique walked in and looked around. "I see my boys have been busy."

The demon spawn looked at each other. Oh, boy.

CHAPTER 7

MOMMA DOMINIQUE

"Momma! What are you doing here?" Carson asked her. To say she scared him was an understatement. Dominique had that effect on her boys.

"You boys need help," she said. "Well, somewhat." She walked over and checked out Gema and Becca. "Hm, you seem promising," she said to Gema. "You." She looked at Becca. "We'll wait and see."

"Momma," Cody said.

"She's mousy." She rolled her eyes. "Why am I hearing you think you're in love with your cousin's fiancée?" She asked Carson.

"I love her, momma," he told her.

Then she slapped him upside the back of the head. "Wake up, shit for brains!"

He rubbed the back of his head.

"Don't be a putz. Maggie is Nash's girl. Get your own girl," she told him.

"You don't understand," he said.

"Oh, stop your whining," Cayson said while walking into the house.

"Hey, Uncle Cayson," Nixon said.

"Hey, Nix. So, what is wrong with my boy? Why does my wife look like she's ready to beat his ass?"

"Well, Carson told her he loves Maggie."

"Boy, did you lose your damn mind?" Cayson asked Carson.

"Whose side are you on?" Carson asked him.

"Well, not yours." He shrugged.

"Oh, that's not even the best part. My friend likes him, but he doesn't like her. She's one of the hottest girls at school," Gema said to them.

"You have lost your damn mind. And who are you?" He asked Gema.

"I'm Gema. Caleb's girl." She grinned.

"I like you." He waved a finger at her.

"I'm Becca. Cody's girl," Becca said.

"I'm not so sure about you." He rolled his eyes.

"Dad!" Cody said.

"Shut up, Cody," Cayson said.

"Okay, I want to meet this Meg," Dominique told them.

They looked at each other as Cayson whispered to Nixon to call me. The shit was about to hit the fan.

*****

Nash and I walked over to a house. We knocked on a door. I got yanked inside by none other than Carson.

"Carson! Thanks for almost ripping my arm out of its socket," I said while rubbing my arm.

"Maggie, you have to save me," he said.

"Save you from what?" I asked until I saw Dominique and Cayson. "Oh."

Then I saw Meg, the other girls, Nixon, Cody, and Caleb. Is it too late to run?

*****

I stood there listening as Meg ranted and raved that Carson thinks he's in love with me. Dominique was not happy. Did I mention they threw each other under the bus?

Yeah, this was fun.

"Okay, okay. Enough!" Dominique said, causing Meg to stop. "I get it. My boy is an idiot. But you shouldn't be taking a random boy to your room."

"Wait. What about Cody and Caleb?" Carson asked her.

"What about them?" She asked while giving him her infamous look. Do you know the one that mothers have that says not to question them? That would be the one.

They signaled to their brother to stop talking. Like a good Gray boy, he didn't.

"Well, they hooked up with their girls on the first day they met them," he told her while throwing them under the bus.

They shot him a glare, and she looked at them as they looked around, whistling.

She sighed, rolled her eyes, and shook her head. "I blame your father for your lack of morals."

"What did I do? I wasn't like Jonas and knocked up a girl I didn't know! We got married!" He spoke.

I placed my palm on my face.

"Still, you boys need to get your shit together," she told them. "You boys should be gentlemen, not jackasses. Women deserve respect and food."

We stopped and looked at her.

"I'm making dinner. You're staying. Nashville, call your brothers, their girlfriends, and your cousins," she told him. "I'm making spaghetti. Then we're going to sit and eat together." She smiled as she made her way to the kitchen.

"Well, you heard my wife," Cayson said as he followed Dominique.

Nash made a call. Meg wasn't happy with Carson, and Carson looked like he wanted to puke. The others, well, they looked like they wanted to be anywhere but here. It would be a long dinner.

*****

Dominique made dinner, and we took our seats. Then she spoke grace because, well, she's a devout Catholic, as is Cayson and their sons. How? I don't know, considering I'm sure that Satan spawned them.

We ate, and Dominique said, "I hope if you're planning on screwing my sons, you're planning on getting married."

We choked on our food. Water, I need water.

"Oh, was it something I said?" She asked.

We took a drink of water from our glass.

"Now, you three." She zeroed in on Meg, Gema, and Becca. "You like my sons, right?"

Gema and Becca agreed. Meg, not so much.

"I did until I found out he's a jackass." She glared at Carson.

"Wait. What?" Carson asked her.

"You heard me, deaf boy. You left me hanging. I should leave you hanging."

"No. You can't do that."

"I did. I don't like you." Meg smirked.

"Well, I don't like you."

"And I don't like you."

"Yeah, well, you're an idiot."

"You're a twit."

"You're a tool."

"And you're so freaking hot right now."

"Yeah, well, you're so, so." He tried to find the words which were escaping him.

"I'm what?"

They stood, leaning across the table. The unthinkable happened as Carson pulled Meg to him. Then they started making out, landing right onto the table.

"I lost my appetite," Jaime said.

"And my work here is done." Dominique smirked as she continued eating.

"Hey, you two over there, sucking face. Do you want to take this somewhere else?" Cayson asked. Jace grabbed Carson and yanked him off the table, while Nash pulled Meg off the table.

"I still don't like you," she said to him.

"That's fine because I'll show you how much I don't like you." He smirked.

That was the most grotesque thing I had ever seen. Wait. No. Nash and I kissed after throwing food at each other. I would say I have seen more odd things. Wait. Did I say Nash and I had our first kiss after a food fight?

I thought about it, and it hit me. Whoa.

"What is it?" Nash asked me.

"We had our first kiss at breakfast after a food fight."

A smile curled upon his lips. "You remember."

"I remember." I smiled.

"What's with the two of you and your sickening smiles?" Nixon asked us.

"Oh, nothing," he said. "Maggie remembered our first kiss."

The boys smiled when he told them.

"What?" Brook asked Nolan.

"Maggie lost her memory a year and a half ago," Nolan told her. "She lost over two years of her life. A quack doctor tried to kill her."

Everyone went silent as Brook said, "Oh."

I sat there. The mere mention of that doctor upset me.

"You'll get your memory back, right?" Becca asked me.

"No," I said.

Nash placed his hand on mine. "Hey, it's okay. Remember, it's you and me together forever."

I nodded as tears fell from my eyes. It was still hard knowing someone wanted to end your life on purpose. I was lucky to lose my memories. It didn't mean it didn't hurt any less.

"Excuse me." I got up from the table as Nash followed suit.

"Is she still having a hard time?" Cayson asked the brothers.

"It's gotten better, but the minute we mention this, she feels like it's happening again," Nixon told him.

"Dad, it was scary watching her go through it," Carson said to him.

"Yeah, she didn't know who any of us were. She knew she stayed with the Grays," Cody said.

"But Maggie is a strong person. It would be best if you boys gave her more credit," Dominique said.

"I guess so but having to watch what happened to her. It scared the shit out of us," Nathan said to her.

Everyone looked at each other. My experience had left a lasting impression on everyone.

*****

I stood outside and wiped my face as two muscular arms slid around me. I didn't need to ask who it was. My heart knew.

I laid my head back onto his chest as he held me. We said nothing but stood there. As Nash said, we didn't need words because it was him and me forever.

I wasn't sure about everyone else. With school getting ready to start, this year will become exciting. Can we make it to the wedding?

CHAPTER 8

HATE IS SUCH A, UM, WELL, NEVER MIND

After the dinner with the demon spawn and their parents, school started with a bang. It happened with Meg and Carson. If they weren't arguing, they were making out. It was beyond weird.

Nash and I met up with Nolan and Brook to have lunch after class when Carson caught up with us.

"Yo, cuz. What's up?" Nolan asked him.

"I need advice," he said.

"About what?" Nash asked.

"Meg," he said.

"I'm out," he said as I giggled.

Carson looked at him. "Thanks?"

Nash shrugged as he pulled me close. Coward.

"Come on, guys! I need advice," he said.

"How about not being a douche?" Brook asked him. He gave her a look as we tried to stifle a laugh.

"Okay, okay." Nolan chuckled. "What do you need?"

"How do I make Meg my girl?" He asked Nolan.

"What do you mean, how do you make her your girl? Don't you know?" Nolan gave him a strange look.

"I know. Well, until things got screwed up," Carson said.

We looked at him like he was a certifiable idiot. Oh, wait. He's an idiot as I shook my head at him. What is wrong with these boys? Are they serious?

"You mean you screwed things up," Brook said.

"No, that's not what I mean," he said.

"And pray tell, what do you mean? I'm curious to know how you didn't screw things up. Remember when you said you were in love with Maggie but had mommy set you straight," Brook said.

Carson glared at her until Nolan got between Brook and Carson. He looked at Brook. "You stop," he told her.

"Or what?" She asked him.

"Or you'll find out later what punishment I have in store for you." He smirked. Brook clamped her mouth and turned three shades of red. Yeah, I don't even want to know what he had planned for her.

Nolan turned to Carson. "Well, she has a point. You screwed things up. I'm surprised that Nash didn't string you up and beat the living shit out of you."

"Nolan."

"But being the exceptional cousin I am, I'll tell you how to land Meg. Don't screw it up." He shrugged.

"Fine."

"Okay, first things first, you need to eat crow. Kiss her ass. Be Meg's bitch," he said, with Nash nodding in agreement. "You kiss her ass a lot. Well, scratch that. There's never enough ass-kissing you can do for the shit you have pulled."

"Nolan," Carson spoke through gritted teeth.

"Hey. Do you want my advice or not?"

"Fine."

"Now, once you kiss her ass, then you want to nail her." He grinned. Wait. What? Nash placed his face in his palm.

"Huh?" Carson cocked his head at Nolan, as did the rest of us.

"Dude, Meg appears to be this proper girl in public, but she's a freak behind closed doors."

"How do you know?"

We looked at Carson as Nixon walked up. "What are you guys talking about?"

"Oh, Nolan is giving Carson love advice about Meg," Nash told him.

"Good luck," Nixon said.

"Nolan is saying Meg is a freak behind closed doors. I should nail her. I don't even know how he would know," Carson told Nixon.

Nixon arched an eyebrow at Carson. "Nolan? Were you dropped on your head as a baby? Do you realize it's Nolan we are talking about here?" Nixon gave Carson a look.

"Oh." Carson thought about it as they looked at him, then said, "Ohh."

The boys smirked at him. If it was one thing Nolan prided himself on, it's sex. That was one thing you could not deny about him. Even his brothers knew that about him.

"So, what you're saying is to wine and dine her, then nail her?" Carson asked.

"No, I'm saying you need to kiss her ass then nail her. Pay attention," Nolan said.

Carson looked at everyone who stared back. As much as I hate to say it, Nolan had a point. What was it? Again, I didn't want to ask. He was the guy who took my bras when he was fifteen.

"Okay, fine, but if this blows up in my face, I'll kick your ass." Carson turned and walked away.

"Do you think it'll work?" Nixon asked them.

"You got me. Carson's desperate, and it's fun to mess with him." Nolan grinned as we started laughing.

*****

Carson followed Nolan's advice. Boy, he kissed Meg's ass, which was way out of character for him. He went back to her room with her, following through with said advice.

It got crazy between them. Before Carson and Meg knew it, the clothes were off. He had her bent over a dresser while going at it.

They went at it until both collapsed on the bed, exhausted.

She rolled over and looked at him. "Well, that's a start."

He turned to her. "I want you as my girl."

She arched an eyebrow. "What if I don't want to be your girl?"

He got up and pinned her to the bed. "Then, I guess I can punish you until you agree."

"I like to see you do your worst." She smirked. And Carson did his worst. It took much convincing, but she relented and agreed to be his girl. How do I know this? Because I got to hear about it when he told the boys. I'll kill Nash.

Yeah, he figured if he had to suffer, so did I. Jerk.

The triplets settled down with a girl. It was nauseating here, and I thought the boys were bad. We had an issue with Jace and Jaime trying to meet someone.

The problem was they would meet someone. It wouldn't be without a few obstacles along the way. Yeah, that would happen at a party.

We had to deal with these relationship issues and wedding planning. We were getting married after graduation. Why, may you ask? I guess Nate and Pat wanted us out of the house.

I couldn't blame them. I mean, the quicker Nate and Pat could get us out of the house, the faster they could dwindle to an empty nest. I wanted to graduate college while trying to avoid everyone's issues, get married, and start my life as Mrs. Nash Gray. We had to figure out where we would live. Ugh, I need a vacation from life.

CHAPTER 9

BACK-TO-SCHOOL PARTY

Marco, Jasper, and Paul threw a back-to-school party. Everyone went. Since most of us were with someone, we attended with our significant others. Jaime was looking to hook up with someone, dragging his brother along for the ride.

We arrived and mingled. Nash and I stayed glued to each other the entire night. While the others were doing their own thing, Jaime and Jace hung with us. Two girls walked up.

"Cool party," one girl said to Jaime.

"Yeah, it's decent," he said.

"I'm Briana, and this is my sister, Andi."

"I'm Jaime, and this is my brother, Jace, cousin Nash and his fiancée, Maggie."

"Nice to meet you." She shook our hands.

We started talking. Bri was a senior like us and graduating this spring. Her sister Andi was in town visiting her and checking out colleges.

"So, Jace, is it?" Andi asked Jace.

"Yeah," Jace said.

"So, you're a senior, huh?"

"Yeah, I am." He tried to act casual.

"That is so cool." She smiled as Jace smiled back. Hmm, it looks like Jace's smitten.

We talked as Jace and Jaime danced with Bri and Andi. They seem like likable girls.

Nash and I continued to talk as the party got into full swing. My phone rang. We went outside so that I could answer it. It had something to do with the wedding.

While we were outside talking, things got interesting inside. Andi kissed Jace, but he pulled away. "Whoa," he said.

"What's wrong?" She asked him.

"Dancing is one thing, but nothing more."

"Why?"

He stopped and ran his hand through his hair. "Because you're seventeen, and I'm twenty-three. That is why. Excuse me." He walked away as she stood there, defeated. Jaime and Bri stopped dancing and talked to her.

"What did I do wrong? I mean, he seems to be into me," she said with furrowed brows.

"It's not you. Jace always does the right thing," Jaime said.

"Oh." She turned and walked away.

"Great." Bri sighed.

"What's going on?" Jaime asked her.

"Andi has a hard time with guys. She came here to get away from things at school. Jace is the first guy to show a genuine interest in her."

Jaime looked at her, then at Andi.

He turned to her. "My aunt and uncle are seven years apart. If they can make it work, so can they."

"Huh?"

"Follow me. I have an idea."

She nodded as they went to find a brother. Nash and I stood on the porch when someone came flying past us while crying. Andi?

"Pat, can we call you back later?" I asked as I hung up.

"What was that about?" Nash asked me.

"I don't know. It can't be good."

Bri came out of the house without Jaime. "Did you see my sister?"

"Yeah, she went that way. What's going on?" Nash asked her.

"Andi thought Jace took an interest in her, and he rejected her," she told us.

Nash and I looked at her, then at each other. Then Jaime came out with Nixon.

"Now what?" Nash asked.

"Our cousin has morals," Nixon said.

"Well, she is seventeen," Nash said.

"So? Maggie was seventeen when you two got together," he said.

"Yeah, but you know, Jace. He's not that guy," Nash said.

"It doesn't matter. I know my brother," Jaime told them.

"What do you mean?" Nash asked Jaime.

"Nash, he was into this girl, but when she kissed him, his brain kicked into overdrive. He's concerned about the age difference," Jaime told us.

Nash, Nixon, and I looked at each other. Well, damn.

Jaime and Bri searched for Andi. We went looking for Jace. It took time to find him, but we found him. He was out back, alone.

Nash walked over to him. "Jace?"

"Nash, I don't need you to start with me," he said without looking at Nash.

Nash walked over and stood next to him. "So, is it the six years age difference that bothers you, or are you scared to let someone in?" Nash shot him a glance as Jace glanced at him and sighed.

"Nash, I don't know what to do. There's something about this girl, but she's seventeen and still in high school. I'm graduating and going to be settling down." He shook his head.

"Well, what about waiting?"

"Huh?"

"Dad waited until Ma was eighteen. Wait until she turns eighteen, then go for it."

"I don't know, Nash." He shook his head.

The three of us looked at each other. The brothers started planning. What could go wrong? Everything.

We went back to the house. I had gotten tired. We walked in, and I walked over to the couch, plopping on it. Nash joined me on the couch as the others made their way inside, taking a seat.

"So, let me get this straight. Jace likes someone in high school but can't get his shit together," Nathan said.

"Pretty much," Nash said.

"Well, he's a dumbass," Noah said.

"Well, I can see his point," I said.

"How so?" They asked me.

"Think about it. Andi is a senior in high school. She doesn't have the experiences that everyone else has. He doesn't want to take her chances away from her," I said.

They looked at me, then Nixon asked, "Have you lost your damn mind?"

We looked at him.

"No, she lost her memory, dude," Nolan said.

I shot Nolan a look as he shrugged.

"Our cousin is a dipshit. He needs a chick. If she is young, then so be it," Nixon said.

I placed my palm on my face. Yep, there was no reasoning with the boys when they started plotting and planning.

So much for trying to get through my senior year without issue. Did I mention we had to get through wedding planning and school? Can someone shoot me now?

While the brothers plotted and planned, I went upstairs to go to bed. The situation exhausted me. Nash came up a few minutes later. He changed before crawling into bed with me.

He pulled me to him, then started giving me kisses. Even though I'm tired, I couldn't resist his lips. Before I knew it, our clothes were on the floor. Nash took extra time with me, going slow with me.

With everything that was happening, being here with him was worth it. It was us, together, and he always took great care of me.

After we finished, I laid in his arms. "Did I mention Dad offered me a job after graduation?"

I propped myself. "Doing what?"

"Designing body styles. That way, I can put my artistic ability to use." He smiled.

"I'm glad." I smiled. "Since you have a job lined up, now I have to figure out what I am doing after we graduate." I sighed.

"Well, you might be busy."

"How so?" I arched an eyebrow at him.

"Well, I figure we could start a family." He smirked.

I couldn't help but laugh. "Oh?"

"Yes."

I smiled at him and shook my head while rolling my eyes. "Nash, I want to do something different from having babies."

"Okay, how about this? You like to bake. Why not do something like that?"

I never thought about it. I was taking culinary classes because I like to cook. Plus, I could get creative. Then it hit me.

"I have a better idea." I gave him a mischievous smile.

He gave me a side glance. It was risky. I knew Nash would take the job with his dad to make sure he could support us. His decision wouldn't make him happy. Why not do something together? He could still be artistic, and we could do something we both enjoy.

CHAPTER 10

KISS HER, YOU TOOL

Saturday proved to be an exciting day, woken up by much commotion. I dressed, coming downstairs to the brothers and Jaime talking. I don't want to know. Or do I? Eh, what the heck? It should liven up our Saturday.

"Okay, so it's set. Meet us at this address, and we'll do the rest," Nathan said.

"Are you sure it'll work?" Jaime asked him.

"Look who you're talking to, Jaime. It's us. It'll work," Noah said.

"What will work?" I asked them.

They turned to see me standing there.

"Nothing," Nolan said.

I walked over to Nash. "Your plan involves a particular girl and Jace, right?"

He looked at me while his brothers and cousin looked at him. I didn't even have to wait for an answer. I knew.

"We won't go to jail, will we?"

Nash smirked at me. Great.

*****

We ended up at the park. Bri walked up with Andi while we were waiting, then Jamie arrived with Jace. The minute Jace saw Andi, he stopped and looked at Jaime. "What is this?"

"It's a chance for you to be happy," Jaime said.

"Jaime, I don't need to have you meddle in my love life."

"Oh, I would do no such thing."

Jace pursed his lips.

"They would." He pointed at the brothers.

I looked at Andi, who fidgeted as Bri tried to reassure her. Then it hit me.

"Andi, can we talk?" I asked.

She looked at me as did the others, and she nodded. We walked away, so we could talk without five meddling brothers listening to our conversation.

"What did you want to talk about?" She asked me.

"You got hurt by a boy in school, right?"

She said nothing, but her look said it all.

"I'm guessing you liked this boy, but he didn't like you back?"

She averted her eyes. "Yes."

"So, tell me what happened."

"I had a crush on someone. The guy turned around and laughed in my face." As she talked, I waved the boys over to us. Yeah, I was as bad as them. "I don't even know what I did, but since then, he has made it his mission to make me feel like dirt. I don't understand why."

Before I answered, someone else did. "Because the guy is a tool."

"What?" She asked.

I pointed behind her. She turned, coming face to face with Jace and the others. He strolled towards her as she stood there. I ducked past them, making my way over to Nash.

"I said he was a tool," he said as he reached her. "You're a sweet girl. Any guy would be lucky to have you."

"Not you."

"It's not that."

"Then, what is it? I'm sure you felt something when we kissed because I know I did."

"Andi, you have many things to do and see. I'm getting ready to settle down. I don't want to hold you back."

"I can wait."

"What?"

"I can wait. I did it for four years with a guy I liked. What are another four or five years?" She smiled, letting hope fill her face.

"Andi."

She cut him off. "Jace. I like you because you're different from most guys. You could have been like most guys and gone further with that kiss. You didn't. I admire that." It was a bold move, but one that Jace needed to hear.

"I don't know." He shook his head.

"What's stopping you, Jace? To take a chance and be happy?" She reached out and took his hand. "I know you think it's a big deal with our ages, but it isn't to me."

He looked at her hand as she held his. He rubbed his thumb across her delicate fingers. The warmth that radiated from her was undeniable. For being only seventeen, she seemed so much older. It was an attraction he could not deny.

He lifted his head, looking into her eyes. Her chestnut eyes matched her hair as a twinkle danced in her eyes. It was something he had never seen before with anyone.

"Jace, we can take it slow. With you here and me there, we don't have to worry about anything happening." She smiled. He chuckled, then moved a strand of wavy hair behind her ear.

We stood there and watched them as Nixon said, "Kiss her, you tool!"

They both stopped and looked at him. "Way to ruin a moment, Nix!" Jace said.

I couldn't help but giggle.

"Well, Jace's taking too long. If he keeps this up, he'll turn eighty before asking her out for a date," he said.

"So, Jace likes to take his time." Jaime shrugged.

"Dude, he likes to take more than his time. I have a pet snail that moves faster than he does."

"When did you get a snail?"

The boys started laughing until Jaime realized they had had him. He's a Gray and should know they're fair game.

"Oh, haha." He rolled his eyes.

We stopped and saw Jace and Andi staring at us. Whoops. That's when I helped them out and made everyone turn around, so our backs were facing them.

"Why are our backs to them?" Noah asked me.

"Privacy," I said.

"Oh, right. That makes sense with us being in a park, out in the open, where everyone can see. But let's give them privacy," Nathan said while rolling his eyes.

"Well, could you kiss someone if everyone was staring at you?" I asked him.

They looked at me.

"Never mind," I sighed.

While we had our backs to them, Jace turned to Andi. He looked at her as she looked at him with anticipation. He licked his lips. Jace placed his hand on her cheek, taking great care of her. Then he leaned down as his lips met hers.

With a slight hesitation on both their parts, they shared a kiss. Jace pressed his lips to hers as she reciprocated. She wrapped her arms around his neck while standing on her tippy toes.

It didn't take long for him to wrap his arms around her. He lifted her off the ground, so she didn't have to struggle with the kiss. They pulled back, trying to catch their breaths as their hearts raced. It was a kiss like no other.

He placed his forehead against hers as he said, "Slow is good. Slow is perfect."

She smiled at him.

He set her back down and took her hand. "Okay."

"Okay, what?" She asked him.

"We'll try it, but on one condition."

"What's that?"

"We don't go any further than kissing and hand-holding until you turn eighteen."

She looked at him as we walked up.

"Is that a problem?" He asked.

"What's the problem?" Bri asked them.

"Well, Jace will try it," Andi said, motioning between the two of them. "On one condition. He said, only kissing and hand-holding until I turn eighteen."

Bri laughed, confusing the rest of us.

"What's so funny?" Jaime asked her.

"Andi won't be eighteen until next June." She giggled. We looked at each other, then at Andi as she nodded.

"These next ten months will be a long ten months," Jace said, making Andi giggle. She wrapped her arms around him and stood on her toes to kiss him.

"Look at it this way. You're following in Ma and Dad's footsteps." Nash snickered.

"Don't remind me." Jace sighed.

"Well, if it makes you feel better, we'll still have breaks to see each other," Andi said.

He shrugged and wrapped his arms around her. "That's fine because if anyone messes with my girl, they'll deal with me."

"And the rest of us," Nolan said.

She looked at them, and I said, "Yep, it's true. The Gray boys are overprotective of their women."

Nash wrapped his arm around my waist and pulled me to him. "See what I mean." I smirked.

Andi giggled as Bri looked at Jaime. "Does that go for you too?"

"Of course, doll," he said, pulling her to him as he crashed his lips into hers.

The wedding will be exciting with everyone and their significant others. I didn't know how exciting it would be.

CHAPTER 11

RETRO DANCE: A HALLOWEEN CHAPTER

For Halloween, the school was having a retro dance. Everyone dressed up from whatever decade they wanted. We couldn't choose the 2000s. Nash and I dressed in the 50s style. Everyone else chose different decades, ranging from the 20s to the 90s. The clothing choices were stylish.

Andi came to attend with Jace, so she could spend time with him and her sister. They dressed from the 20s while the demon spawn dressed from the 30s along with their girls. Nathan and Noah dressed from the 40s, while Nixon dressed from the 60s and Nolan dressed from the 80s. Jaime and Bri chose the 70s.

It was unique to see everyone dressed from different eras. Wearing a poodle skirt was interesting. Nash was lucky. He got to wear jeans, a white tee-shirt, and black shoes. Although the tee-shirt made him look hot, the black leather jacket made him look even sexier.

"Mags?"

"Yeah?"

"Are you going to stop drooling, so we can head to the dance?" He smirked.

I looked at Nash as the rest looked at me. "I was not drooling. I was admiring how well Nash wears a leather jacket."

"Uh-huh, sure." He smirked.

"It takes a lot for someone to pull off the leather look," I told him while putting my hand up.

"I'll remember that for later." He winked.

Oh, damn. My heart had stopped.

"Can you putz drool later or some shit? I want to get to the dance before it's over," Nixon said.

"Are you a bit testy there, brother?" Nash asked him.

"I'm always testy. Now let's go."

We snickered. Nixon was always impatient with things. Imagine when he has a kid. Come on, junior, be born now. Poor Kat.

We made our way to the dance. I hope it goes off without a hitch, but I doubt it. One can dream, can't they?

We walked in and made our way to the dance floor, then started dancing. Things were going well until some guys cornered Andi and Gema. That was a colossal mistake. Huge.

"Hey, sweet things," one guy said to the girls, his tone oozing with sleaze.

"Excuse us. We are with our guys," Gema said.

"Yeah, well, not for long." Another guy smirked.

Andi moved closer to Gema as one guy tried to grab her. Well, until Gema smacked him across the face.

"Get your hands off her!" She said, trying to defend her.

"You know, someone needs to teach you manners," another guy said while grabbing her.

"Caleb!" Gema said as she struggled with the aggressive guy.

It took yelling for Gema to alert the boys. That was never good when a guy manhandled a Gray boy's woman.

"Is there a problem here?" Nash asked the guys. The five guys turned to see the Gray brothers and cousins standing there along with their dates.

"Yeah, but we're handling it." One guy smirked.

"Yeah, I don't think so," Jace said.

"Why is that?" Another guy asked him.

"The girl you are trying to paw is my girl, and the girl you mistreated is his girl." Jace pointed at Caleb, who was seething. "Now we'll do it the easy way or the Gray way. It's your choice."

The guys looked at each other. Yep, things were about to get ugly.

*****

Now you must ask yourself why anyone would choose the Gray way. Haven't they heard of the brothers? Have they been living under a rock? Yep, they have.

Fists started flying as the boys went to town, causing a massive fight to break out. It took school officials along with campus security to break up the brawl.

We stood in the Dean's office with our hair a mess, our clothes ripped, and a few had bloody noses and lips.

"This is not being an adult. We do not fight at the school," the Dean told everyone. "You want to fight. I suggest you go back to high school. You're grown adults and need to act like it." We stood there as she lectured us. "Now, since no one can control themselves at a simple school dance. You're on probation for the rest of the semester."

Everyone groaned.

"Do not make me call your parents. I'm sure they wouldn't like to hear how their adult children are acting like two-year-old's," she said.

Then someone entered the office. We turned to see an older woman with silver hair walking towards us. She checked us over. "This seems familiar."

We looked at her, then at each other.

"Hello, Kate," the Dean said.

"Dean," Kate said.

"The students decided it would be a superb idea to fight."

The woman looked at us and chuckled, surprising the Dean.

"What's so funny?" The Dean asked.

"Oh, Taylor, my nephews have done worse. At least, there wasn't punch involved this time. Now, who started it?" She asked us.

"They did," Gema said, pointing at the five guys in question.

She looked at them, eyeing them up and down. "I thought so. You boys have been causing many problems."

"We wanted to talk," a guy said to her.

"Uh, huh. Then why are these boys upset?" She pointed at the brothers and cousins.

"We can't help it if they are overprotective and jealous," another guy said.

"Right. You thought you would challenge these boys. I see. Well, I wonder what my nephews would say if you wanted to talk to their girls?" She shrugged.

The look on the guys' faces spoke volumes. What were they scared of? Because I'm sure they had lost their colorings.

Kate turned to the Dean. "Okay, this is what will happen. You'll call their parents." She pointed at the five boys. "And inform them, we have expelled their sons for starting a riot. Then you'll take everyone off probation because they had nothing to do with it. Why blame everyone for a few? It's their get-out-of-jail-free card."

The Dean and faculty members escorted the five boys away. Jace wrapped his arms around Andi, and Caleb pulled Gema close to him.

The woman smiled at us.

"Okay, this woman is creeping me out," Nixon said to Nash in a low voice.

She turned to Nixon. "You must be the one who gave my nephew Frazier a hard time in the store."

Frazier?

"Oh, great," he said.

The woman chuckled.

"Who's Frazier?" I asked them.

They looked at me, then at each other. Nixon said, "We met him in the store when we were Christmas shopping before you got sick."

"Oh," I said.

"You must be Maggie," she said.

I knitted my brows.

"Alex told me about you. I heard what had happened. I'm sorry you had to go through that."

"Bad things happen to good people, right?" I tried to let it roll off my back, but it was hard. I had such a rough time trying to find my way back.

"Oh, no, honey. I wouldn't think of it that way. Sometimes, unpleasant things happen, but pleasurable things come from it," she said. "It's what you do with that second chance that counts." She gave me a warm smile and a wink.

She made sense.

"Plus, you never know when you'll need a friend." She smiled again and then walked away. I wondered what she meant.

"I don't know about you, but I'm ready to go home and take a shower," he said to me as he touched his lip.

I turned and checked his mouth as he hissed through his teeth. "Oh, stop being a baby." I examined his lips.

"Mags, it freaking hurts!"

"Oh, wah."

We started bickering.

"Those two will be interesting once they get married. Maggie and Nash sound like Ma and Dad," Noah told the others.

"Yep," Nixon, Nathan, and Nolan said.

We headed back to the house. I needed a shower. Plus, we watched scary movies in honor of Halloween. I think dances aren't our thing. Something always goes wrong.

Nash and I took a shower together and washed up. While he was washing my back, I thought about what Kate said. Sometimes, we need a friend. What was that supposed to mean?

"Mags?"

"Yeah?"

"Are you okay?"

"Yeah, I'm thinking about my future."

His hands moved to my hair as he washed it. "I hope it includes me."

"I'm sure you're a big part of it." I glanced at him. "I'm thinking about what you said the other night, and I was thinking."

"About?"

"Combining the two things we enjoy."

He arched an eyebrow at me as I smiled. I knew it was a gamble, but it would work. We need to work out the finer details.

We finished up and got dressed, joining everyone else for a horror film marathon. I don't know why I subject myself to this, considering how I scare easily. Nash was good with me jumping into his lap, considering he held me tight. Ladies and gentlemen, my fiancé is a dirty boy.

Tonight, I won't get any sleep in more ways than one. Oh, boy.

CHAPTER 12

WEDDING DECISIONS

After the Halloween fiasco, Nash and I were getting bombarded with wedding decisions. They could do whatever they wanted. All I wanted to do is show up.

I laid on the bed and stared at the ceiling. Nash walked in and climbed on top of me, hovering over me. "The ceiling will still be there, no matter how hard you stare at it."

"I know." I sighed.

"What's wrong, baby girl?"

"Is it weird that I don't care what they decide about the wedding?"

He gazed at me.

I wrapped my arms around his neck. "All I want to say is I do."

A smile curled upon his lips as he kissed me. Then my phone rang. We sighed. Please, let it not be about the wedding. I saw a random number and answered it. "Hello?"

The person started speaking, and I said, "No, I don't want to buy any magazines." I hung up. I hate solicitors.

My phone rang again, and I answered it. "I said I don't want your stupid magazines!"

It's an excellent thing that I'm not selling magazines. Someone chuckled.

"I'm sorry. Who is this?"

Kate Jones.

My eyes widened as I put her on speaker so Nash could hear too.

I'm wondering if it would interest you to learn about baking.

This woman surprised me since I didn't even know her.

The professors have told me brilliant things about you. They said you have a talent for baking and cooking. I want to cultivate that.

I had never given it much thought until Nash mentioned it. I took culinary and baking classes so I could cook for us without killing us. It would be great if Nash didn't have to have his stomach pumped.

What do you say, Maggie?

I glanced at Nash as he nodded in agreement.

"Sure. That sounds great," I said.

Good. You'll intern with me starting tomorrow.

She hung up, and I stared at Nash, shocked. That was surreal. I would have never thought someone would call, offering me an internship.

"Well, I guess you know what you'll do for a career. I won't have to worry about your cooking killing me." Nash smirked.

I smacked him with a pillow. As we laughed, he went to kiss me until we heard yelling. Now, what was going on?

We made our way downstairs.

"Is it my fault your girl doesn't have a sense of humor?" Carson asked Cody.

"That was bullshit, and you know it!" Cody said.

"Why did you tools have to come here to yell at each other? Couldn't you have done that at your place?" Nixon asked them.

"Considering jackass here pulled a prank on Becca. No. I'm moving out!" Cody said.

"And where are you moving to?" Nash asked him.

"I was thinking here." Cody grinned.

"Yeah, no," Nathan said.

"Why not? You guys have room!"

"Because no offense, we don't want you here," Nathan said.

"But I'm family!" He spoke.

"And you have other families you could live with," Noah said.

"Come on, guys. Becca won't even talk to me unless I move in here."

There it was.

"Why does it have to be us?" Nolan asked him. The rest of us watched Cody with curiosity.

"Because, according to her, she likes you guys. She said you had done nothing wrong to her," he said.

Was Cody for real? Does this girl know what the brothers will do to her?

The brothers glanced at each other and smirked. Oh, no. I know that look. That's a look that says I'm a Gray. You're about to have your ass handed to you.

"Okay, you can stay. We would love to get to know your little girlfriend better." Nixon smirked.

"Great! Later, losers," he said to his brothers as he left.

"You realize it has nothing to do with a prank, right?" Carson asked them.

"What do you mean?" I asked him.

"Becca has a thing for them," Caleb added, pointing at the brothers.

I turned to the brothers, but it didn't faze them. Why?

"That's cool. After we finish with Becca, she'll hate us," Nathan said with a smirk.

Carson and Caleb glimpsed at each other. They may be the demon spawn themselves. When the brothers got together, they were worse with outsiders. Trust me. I know.

*****

Cody brought his bags over, getting settled in an empty room. Becca came with him to help as Meg and Gema stopped by.

"I told her this was a terrible idea," Gema told Meg.

"You know Becca. She doesn't listen and only hears what she wants to hear," Meg said.

I walked over to them. "So, does Becca even realize what's coming?"

They both looked at me, and I gave them a look.

"No. Becca thinks she has better access to the brothers with Cody living here," Gema told me.

"And which guy does she have her eye on?" I asked them.

They glanced at each other. The girls didn't need to answer because I knew it was Nash.

"So, what are you going to do?" Gema asked me.

"Nothing." I sighed.

"What do you mean, nothing? If it were me, I would rip a girl's hair out for even looking at my man," Meg said.

"Well, I know the brothers. They don't like it when someone causes trouble for their girls. My bet is on the boys." I shrugged.

Meg and Gema let out a low whistle. Yeah, it wasn't good.

*****

Cody settled in, and Becca was hanging around more. She was in proximity with Nash every chance she could get. The brothers noticed. Cody was freaking oblivious to it. I guess love does crazy stuff to your brain.

At one point, Nixon caught her trying to corner Nash in our bedroom. If Nixon sees you doing something wrong, it's never good.

"Why are you here?" Nixon asked.

Nash and Becca looked at Nixon.

"Oh, I was coming to ask Nash something," she said.

"I don't think asking me to sneak behind my fiancé's back is something," Nash said, reminding her of her stupid question.

She looked like she got caught with her hand in the cookie jar. It's never a good thing.

"Oh," Nixon said. He gave her a look that we knew well.

"Well, she can't do much with him." She pointed to Nash.

"What's that supposed to mean?" Nixon asked her.

"Oh, she needs to get over it. This 'poor me' bit is old. I mean, who lies about losing their memory with Nash. If it were me, I could never forget this fine piece of a specimen," she said, purring.

That made their blood boil, and Nash pushed her aside. "That's where you're wrong. You know nothing about Mags. Accusing her of faking isn't only disrespectful but rude. Don't even talk about my love for her. You know nothing about it." He stormed away as Nixon looked at her.

Her mouth went agape.

"Bad move, sweetheart," he said while turning and walking away.

*****

I came out of class, struggling with my books. Someone grabbed hold of me, crashing their lips into mine. I dropped my books as I kissed the person back.

People stopped and stared at us. Nash pulled back. "You know how much I love you, right?"

"Is this about Becca?"

He cocked his head and squinted his eyes, letting go of me. "You knew."

"Of course, I knew." I crouched and picked up my books with his help.

"Why didn't you say anything?"

We stood up as he handed me a book, and I took it from him. "Why should I?"

"Why the hell not?"

"Because I trust my fiancé, and I know your brothers." I smiled.

He rolled his eyes at me. "Mags, we need to work on you telling me things. I don't want to deal with the aftermath."

"Nash, if I have learned anything, it's to stay out of things with you guys. So, are you going to tell Cody?"

"Nope."

"Why not?"

"Because it's better to deal with things, the Gray way."

I gave him a look as he smirked. Whatever they had planned, I knew it would be crazy. They are the Gray brothers.

CHAPTER 13

DON'T GET MAD GET EVEN, THE GRAY WAY

Have you ever met someone who should leave well enough alone? But the person doesn't and finds out the hard way. Yep, it happened with Becca and the brothers.

People thought what they did to me at the start of senior year was terrible. It's nothing compared to what they did to her. The girls and I walked across campus when we stopped. Our eyes widened as our jaws dropped.

Underwear wasn't hanging on the flagpole, but Becca in her underwear.

"I've got to hand it to them. The boys are getting more ingenious," Kat said.

I glanced at her. Then we ran over to the brothers and Becca as people gathered.

"Nash, what's going on?" I asked Nash.

"Well, since someone enjoys trying to cause trouble, we gave her a taste of her own medicine." He smirked.

"Get me down from here!" She told them.

"Ladies and gentlemen, I give you Becca. She thinks she can try to break up a Gray brother and his girl, even though she's dating a Gray boy. Irony at its best!" Nathan said through a bullhorn. Where did he get a bullhorn?

Noah grabbed the bullhorn. "Now, look at her. You want to stay away from her!"

Then Nixon grabbed it. "Because when you mess with one, you mess with all."

"How's the air, Becca?" Nolan asked as everyone laughed.

"Nash, get her down," I said.

"Why? Because, according to her, you're faking everything," he said.

I looked at him and everyone, including Becca. I stood there speechless as Cody walked up with his brothers.

"She did what?" We heard someone ask.

We turned to see Cody seething.

"It's funny. The girl you admire so much feels my girl is faking everything that happened to her. She made it her quest to break us apart," Nash told him.

I stood there, still speechless.

"You're lying!" Cody told Nash.

"Cody, why would I lie? Think about it. What do I have to gain?" Nash gave Cody a skeptical look.

"Everything, Nash. This stunt is even low for you," he said as he stormed past them and went over to lower Becca. We watched as he helped her down and looked at everyone. "You didn't have to humiliate her. You could have come to me. I guess a lack of respect is the Gray way. Come on, Becca." He led her away as I stood there.

They watched, then turned to me. "I don't understand what I did. How do I make someone think I was faking? Let me tell you. Two years erased from you and getting sporadic memories back is fantastic. I can't remember anything. People trying to tell me is so incredible. Oh, and to have someone try to kill me because their relative had a beef with me. I'm faking everything, right?"

I turned and walked away. I wondered if everyone felt this way. It takes one person to put a shred of doubt in people's minds. I needed to find some perspective. So, I went to see someone who could give it to me.

✶✶✶✶✶

The bell chimed to the bakery, and I looked around. A guy was cleaning up.

"Excuse me. Is Kate here?" I asked the guy.

He turned around and looked at me. He had dark hair with frosted tips and emerald-green eyes. "Nah, Kate left. She had to take care of a few things."

"Oh."

"Wait. I know you."

I stopped. Great, someone else who thinks I'm faking.

"You're that girl with that one guy and his loudmouth brother." He grinned.

Okay, I wasn't expecting that.

I introduced myself. "Maggie."

"Frazier."

So, this was the Frazier everyone mentioned. Interesting.

"I wanted to talk to Kate about something."

"Well, I'm not a gruff silver-haired woman, but I'm good at helping." He grinned.

"I doubt it." I sighed.

"Try me."

It was a challenge. What do I have to lose?

"Fine. People think I'm faking my memory loss."

"Huh, interesting. Now, is it every one or is it one person?"

"What difference does it make?"

"Well, if it's everyone, then I would say sure. If it's one, I would say it's because the person is jealous." He shrugged. "Come. We'll have coffee and talk."

I watched him as he walked towards the counter, then behind it, making two coffees. He returned and sat at a table. He patted a chair next to him. I walked over and took a seat.

"Now, people will always try to come between people. They want what the other person has."

"But that is ridiculous."

"Is it? Think about it. This other person thinks by doing this that they'll achieve what you have. They don't realize what it took for you to get where you're at."

I took a sip of my coffee. "You sound like a psychologist."

"Nah, that is Jordan. I'm a pastry chef. I enjoy making cakes. He enjoys analyzing people." He grinned.

I arched a brow at him.

"I know people. Take my two best friends, Ryan and Alex. Ryan's always screwing up and pissing Alex off. She's so awkward that she hides in the bathroom."

"Why the bathroom?"

"Why not?" He shook his head. "That's not the point of what we're talking about. Other people have tried to break them apart.

They've never succeeded because their love is that strong. I'm guessing your guy handled things his way." He gave me a knowing look.

"But he and his brothers humiliated the girl. They took it too far."

"Did they? The girl didn't listen, and they made her listen."

"Their cousin took her side over theirs."

"He didn't want to admit that his girl isn't as great as she pretends. Insecurity is a bitch." He sipped his coffee.

"Everything is a mess." I sighed.

"Nah, you think it's a mess. But look at the bigger picture. If the guys handle things their way, then that's who they are. My boys handle things with their fists. We handle things our way." He shrugged.

I thought about it. That was true. The Gray boys have always been crazy and did insane shit throughout the years. Why did I expect them to change now? Even though I changed, it doesn't mean they have to.

"You have people who want to talk to you." He pointed at the brothers, who were standing there. I was deep in thought that I didn't hear them come in.

I walked over to them. "How long have you been standing here?"

"Long enough, Mags," Nash said.

"I'm sorry. You guys were doing what you felt was your way of dealing with the situation."

"Maggie, we wondered if we took it too far. Sure, but it's because you're important to us," Noah said.

"We know you aren't faking. We were there as well as the others," Nathan said.

"You're still a pain in the ass, but you're our pain in the ass. Plus, if you guys break up, Ma and Grammy will hurt us," Nixon said.

"Plus, if Cody can't get his head out of his ass to see who his girl is, then that's his problem. But no one, and we mean no one, messes with our sister," Nolan said to me.

I opened my arms as they jumped on me. Yeah, we weren't typical by any means. I have crazy brothers and one insane fiancé, but I wouldn't have it any other way.

"So, what about Cody?" I asked them.

"Eh, screw him. If he wants to be a tool, then let him. He'll find out the hard way." Nixon smirked.

"Trust us. Going against family is never good," Nathan said.

What did these idiots do now?

"Do I even want to know?"

"Nope," they said to me.

Why will the shit hit the fan? Oh, because it's the Grays. Shit always hits the fan.

CHAPTER 14

OH, BOY, HERE WE GO

With everything that had happened, Cody steered clear of everyone. Becca decided she wanted to get even, except one person would stop her. Don't ask.

We were at the house, hanging out, when we heard a knock on the door. Then it became deadly quiet. We looked at each other as another knock sounded.

"Why is no one answering the door?" Meg asked as she walked over to it. We knew she didn't know. Good luck, Meg.

She opened it. "Can I help you?"

"No, but I can help you," the person said.

The person walked in, and it was none other than Grammy Gray.

"Now, where are Cody and his girl? I want a word with them," she told us.

We looked at each other. It's never good when Grammy wants a word with you.

*****

We waited while Carson and Caleb went to retrieve their brother and Becca. She sized up Gema, Meg, and Bri.

"So, you're my grandsons' girls."

"Yes, ma'am," they said.

She walked over to Bri. "Hm." Next was Gema. "Uh, huh?" Finally, Meg. "Huh."

The girls and I stood there while she crossed her arms and tapped her foot. Grammy had put Brook through the drill. We all had to endure her.

"So, what are your intentions with my grandsons?"

"Well, I plan on beating him into submission," Meg told her.

She cocked an eyebrow at her. "Interesting, and you?" She looked at Gema.

"Well, as long as he stays in line, he won't have to worry about me chopping off his balls." She grinned.

"I see, and you?" She glanced at Bri.

"I figure a good right hook should do the trick," she said, balling up her right hand.

Grammy looked at them and smiled. "Good to know you'll take care of them."

We tried not to laugh. You must hold your own with the Gray boys.

A few minutes later, Carson and Caleb returned with Cody and Becca.

Cody saw her and said, "Nope." He tried to leave.

"Cody Mitchell Gray! Don't you dare walk out of this house," she said as he stopped and cursed to himself. "Now, bring your stupid ass and your stupid ass girlfriend over here before I drag you both over here."

They walked over to her. "And who do you think you are?" Becca asked.

No, Becca. You signed your death warrant.

"Well, it was nice knowing her," Nixon said.

"Who will call the funeral director?" Noah asked them.

"I will," Nathan said.

"I'll order the flowers," Nolan said,

"Let's pick out a nice casket for her," Jace said to Nash, who nodded.

"Excuse me. Nah, uh. You don't get to speak. You get to be quiet and listen to me," Grammy told her. She opened her mouth and shut it. "Who the hell do you think you are to cause trouble? Let me tell you that isn't happening, sweet cheeks. You tried to make a play for Nashville, which was the wrong move. Any of these other idiots, be my guest."

"Hey!" The boys said.

"Oh, shut up!" She spoke.

The boys shut up.

"Now to say Margaret was faking. Are you stupid?"

Becca shifted in her spot.

"You listen to me. You either get your shit together and leave Nash and Maggie alone." She pointed at Nash and me. "Or you'll deal with me. If I can try to kill my boy, I sure as hell can take you out. Capeesh?"

Becca nodded.

Grammy turned her attention to Cody. "And you. What the hell is wrong with you?"

"You don't understand, Grammy. They hung her on a flagpole in her underwear," he said.

"So?" She waited for an answer.

"That wasn't right!"

"Coming from one demon spawn himself, don't stand there and lecture me about right and wrong. You, of all people, should know your cousins went easy on her. If it were me, I would have strung her up naked."

Our jaws dropped.

"You never take sides against the family. You're lucky it's me you're dealing with and not your uncles and grandfather."

Our eyes widened. Grayson, Nate, Jonas, and Cayson would have done damage from the stories I had heard.

"Now get your head out of your ass and act like a damn Gray!"

I never saw a Gray boy shake as Cody did. Becca looked like a ghost after the color drained from her face.

"Now that is settled. Let's talk about wedding details," Grammy said, turning to us.

Great. I glanced at Nash as he groaned. It serves him right for calling Grammy.

After enduring an evening with Grammy going over things for the wedding, they gave me one task. I had to make sure I got my wedding dress. The other girls would get their dresses and handle the bachelorette party. The boys would take care of the bachelor party. Nixon was Nash's best man, and Kat was my maid of honor.

Grammy, Pat, and the aunts were handling things back home. Our wedding would be the week after graduation. On the bright side, the girls lived close by us. They would still see the boys after graduation.

Grammy left, and I went upstairs to get something. I heard a knock at the door. I turned to see Becca standing there.

"Maggie, I'm sorry," she said.

I looked at her, annoyed.

"You have this exceptional guy, and I don't think you appreciate him," she said to me.

Her words cut like a knife.

I walked over to her and said, "You don't think I appreciate him."

"Well, yeah. Everyone knows what you put Nash through. He went out of his way for you. You made him feel bad. I know because he told me one night when he stopped by my place."

"What?"

"Yeah, you were having another hissy fit, and he came over. We talked." Becca shrugged.

"You're lying," I spoke through gritted teeth.

"Am I? Because I'm sure, the tat on his shoulder says differently." She smirked.

My heart dropped. Nash had a tat on his shoulder. Few people knew about it except for his family and me and now Becca.

"Excuse me." I walked past her.

She smirked. "Becca 1, Maggie 0."

I walked downstairs and pulled off my ring. I handed it to Nash.

"Mags?".

"I can't compete with others, Nash. Becca told me." Tears fell down my cheeks.

"Told you what?"

"How you stopped over to talk to her, and she knows about your tattoo. While we were together, there was a reason you were on the fence. It's times like these I'm glad I can't remember." I turned and walked out of the house.

"Mags!" He ran after me.

"What the hell is this bullshit?" Nixon asked.

They saw Becca coming downstairs. Cody walked over to her. "What did you do?"

"I told her the truth," she said with an evil look.

"What truth?"

"Nash enjoys other people's company." She smirked.

Meg walked over. "That is a lie."

"Is it?"

"Becca. Nash has never been to our place. He has never spoken to any of us," Gema said to her.

"How do you know? It's not like you or Meg were always around," she said.

Nixon walked over. "Because I know my brother. You say he has a tattoo. What is it?"

"It's an eagle." She smirked.

"Wrong."

Her smirk left her face.

"It's a name. One that belongs to the one he loves. He got it right after they started dating. How do I know? Because I was there. You're a piece of work." Nixon turned to Cody. "Get her out of here before I do some damage." With that, Nixon left.

They glared at her. It was a wrong move on her part.

I heard yelling, but I didn't stop. I didn't understand why. I wanted to marry Nash, but someone always must have their hands in the mix.

Nash and Nixon caught me.

"Stop, Mags!" Nash said.

I whipped around. "Why? I'm not enough. So, the time you tried to reconnect with me when I couldn't remember was what? A joke? Something to kill time with for a while. To clear your conscience?"

"Mags, she's lying. I didn't even know who Becca was until recently."

"How did she know about your tat?"

"I don't know."

"Give me a break, Nash!"

"Maggie, she found out from Cody. It doesn't mean she knows what kind of tat," Nixon said.

"What?" I said, knitting my brows.

"I asked her what tat it was? She said it was an eagle," he said with a knowing look.

"Eagle? Nash doesn't have an eagle. He has my name tattooed on his shoulder," I said.

"Exactly," Nixon said as he gave me a knowing look.

Oh, God. I felt like an idiot. Nash grabbed my hand and took the engagement ring, sliding it back onto my ring finger.

"Woman, you and I will have a serious talk later," Nash told me.

"How serious?" I cringed.

"Let's say you'll have trouble walking for the next week." He smirked.

Oh, God.

"Now come on. We have unfinished business to deal with."

I started walking when he hauled off and smacked my ass. Is it weird that it excited me?

CHAPTER 15

RULE NUMBER 1: NEVER MESS WITH A GRAY BROTHER

We walked into the house. Oh, good. Becca was still here.

I walked over and balled up my ring hand, letting it rip. I cracked her right in the nose, causing her to scream and the boys to say, "Damn!"

"Get out of my house! Stay away from my fiancé! I'm done with your bullshit!"

She grabbed her nose as blood flowed from it. "You broke my nose!"

"And I'll break something else, too. You don't get it. You know nothing about Nash and me. You weren't there. He was. After I almost died, he stayed. If he wanted to cheat on me or leave me, he would have done it a long time ago, but he didn't."

Everyone watched us.

"You wanted Cody. So, why isn't he good enough?"

"That is a good question." We heard someone say. We turned to see Cody walking over to us. "Because of you, I moved out of my brothers' house. Because of you, I wasn't talking to my family. All because of what? You thought by getting closer to Nash, you could break them up, and he would come running to you."

We looked at Cody as hurt flooded his face. He liked Becca.

"Cody," she said to him while holding her nose.

"Save it. I'm done," Cody said as he turned and left. Carson and Caleb went after him as she whimpered.

She went towards Gema and Meg while holding her nose and asked, "Gema? Meg?"

"Becca, what happened to you? Why would you do this?" Meg asked her. She opened her mouth as Meg said, "Forget it." She turned and walked away.

"Gema?"

"Becca, was it worth it? Not only were you trying to come between Nash and Maggie, but you hurt Cody. Pretty sucky, if you asked me." She shrugged and walked away.

We stood there as she looked at us. She had done the damage. If Becca had another chance with Cody, she would need to eat many crows.

She walked out of the house, and Jaime closed the door. Anger filled me. I wasn't so mad at her as I was at myself. When she said that, I assumed. It took Nixon to ask the obvious question. Why a kind of tat?

I walked over and sat on the couch. Was this how I was before? I was unreasonable and running off upset.

Nash walked over and sat next to me.

"I'm sorry." It's all I could manage.

"Well, that's a first." He snickered.

"What is?"

"You're apologizing." He smirked.

"I take it I never did?"

"No, but then again, it was me doing something stupid. Why did we break up? Well, you broke up with me."

He took my hand that held my engagement ring upon it. "This right here." He touched the ring. "I will fit with a band one day. That band will symbolize our commitment and love to each other."

I looked at my hand as he held it, rubbing the pad of his thumb over it. I knew that with us, that's where his heart lies.

"Now, it entitles you to a punishment." He got up and took my hand. He pulled me up and dragged me upstairs.

"Can we talk about it?" I asked as the others chuckled.

"I'll call Andi and fill her in on what's going on," Jace said before leaving.

"Yeah, we're going to go," Jaime said, grabbing Bri's hand and leaving.

The others went along with their business.

Once we reached our room, Nash picked me up and carried me inside, closing the door with his foot. He tossed me onto the bed, then kicked his shoes off and climbed onto it.

I scooted back. Nash grabbed my ankles, pulling off my shoes and tossing them onto the floor. Then he crawled over and hovered over me. He leaned down and pressed his lips to mine.

We pulled at each other's clothes as they went flying, landing on the floor. Nash grabbed protection and rolled it on, then slid inside me. His thrusts started slow, then became fast as he continued. Damn, this was hot.

He let the animalistic quality come out as he went to town. We both felt our release. Then he waited a few minutes before going again, changing positions. That happened pretty much all night. He wasn't kidding when he said I wouldn't be able to walk. I felt dead when we stopped.

If this was his punishment, then he could punish me anytime.

Afterward, I laid on his chest as he wrapped his arms around me. "So, was this your punishment?" I asked him.

His chest shook. "Pretty much."

"I like your punishment." I giggled.

"Mags, you're a naughty girl." He chuckled as I giggled. He rolled over and laid on top of me, looking into my eyes. "When we fought or weren't together, I never once went to another girl."

I knew Nash was still dealing with what had happened. When someone brought it up, he was dealing with it again.

"You went to your brothers."

"Yeah. How did you know?"

"Because if it's one thing I learned about you, Gray boys, your brothers mean everything to you." I smiled.

He smiled and kissed me.

I learned with the brothers that they turned to each other with problems and no one else. Their loyalty was like no other.

As for Becca, I didn't know what would happen to her. She did something you never do. Rule number one is you never mess with a Gray brother. Not only did she mess with one brother, but she hurt another brother in a different family. That was a big fat no.

If I know Cody and his brothers, someone will receive a visit from Momma Dominique. They may be the demon spawn, but family is everything to the Gray women.

It wasn't only Dominique who was coming to pay a visit, but the others. Yep, the original Gray brothers and their wives were showing up to deal with this mess. It was something that would shock everyone.

CHAPTER 16

THE ORIGINAL GRAY BROTHERS ARE COMING; GOD HELP US ALL

The next day, there was a knock on the door. I answered it to find Nate, Pat, his brothers, and their wives standing there. They walked inside.

Nate and Pat hugged me. Nate saw the ring. "Well, the wedding is still on."

"It almost wasn't since baby girl gave me my ring back," Nash said as he walked up and gave Nate and Pat a hug. "What are you doing here?"

"Carson called and told me what happened. He said Ma came to visit, and Becca ignored her warning," Cayson said.

"Does this girl have a death wish?" Jonas asked.

"She has something," Nixon said while walking up and hugging everyone.

"Well, we'll see our boys, then we'll be back," Dominique said. She and Cayson left.

"How bad is it, Dad?" Nash asked Nate.

"It's bad. Cayson said Carson told him that Cody is a mess," Nate said.

"I might be many things, but I wouldn't do something like that," Karen said.

"We'll see the boys and meet up with everyone later. Plus, I have a surprise for Jace," Jonas said to him. He and Karen left to see Jace and Jaime.

"Now, let's fix this before Ma has our heads," Nate told us.

We nodded, and I made a call. After everything that had happened, Becca wouldn't come if we mentioned the name, Gray. So, I called Marco to help. Nothing says sibling love like plotting and planning.

*****

Marco, Jasper, and Paul tricked her into thinking they were going on a double date. It sounded logical. While they went out, they gave us the key to their house. We gathered there and waited.

After a few hours, they returned and went inside. Once inside the darkened room, the door closed, causing Becca to jump. A light flicked on as Nate leaned against the door.

The four of them stood there. Jonas walked in from the left, and Cayson walked in from the kitchen area.

"What is this?" She asked.

"This is us fixing a mess you created." Nate shrugged, standing erect and walking towards her along with his brothers.

"You should know that we don't like when someone uses us," Jonas said.

"Or messes with one of our own," Cayson said, cracking his knuckles.

"If you touch me, I'll scream," she said.

"We won't touch you, but give you a warning," Nate said.

With that, out walked Pat, Karen, and Dominique.

"You want to hurt my boy. I warned you," Dominique spoke. She hauled off and slapped Becca across the face. "How dare you?"

She stared at Dominique while holding her cheek.

"How could you mess with people like that?" Pat asked her.

She looked at Pat, not saying a word.

"Bad move," Karen said.

"I-I," she said.

"You're lucky Maggie hit you because I want to demolish you, even if you only earned a slap from me," Dominique told her. Dominique was protective of the demon spawn and furious. Someone's insensitive behavior hurt one of her children.

"You need to learn a few things to be a part of this family. We don't take kindly to troublemakers. We don't like people who try to wreck things. They think they are smarter than us. Isn't that right, boys?" Nate asked as the boys appeared.

She stared at everyone with wide eyes.

Each set of boys stood by their parents and looked at her.

"See, you forget, these are our boys. We gave them life. We won't let anything happen to them," Pat said.

"We'll love and cherish them until our last breath," Karen said.

"Then we hand them over to the women who deserve them," Dominique said.

Then the rest of us walked out and stood next to our guys, except for Cody. We held each of the boy's hands.

"See, we're loyal, and we expect our women to be loyal to us," Nolan told her.

The boys looked at their women. It was an astounding sight. The Gray boys' love went more profound than the ocean.

Cody walked over to her. "I would have given you everything, but you blew it. The next time you mess with someone, remember this moment. I sure will. Goodbye, Becca," he told her as he turned away from her.

"Cody," Becca said, trying to stop him.

"No, it's over." With that, he walked away.

She stood there as I asked her, "Was it worth it?"

She said nothing except to turn and walk away. I never understood why anyone would want to hurt someone that way. Nash pulled me to him as the others hugged their women.

Dominique and Cayson comforted Cody. They did what any parent would do when their child was hurting. Something told me that Cody would be okay. One day, he would meet that special someone.

I don't think Becca and Cody are over yet. If she gets her shit together, realizing what she has. Nash and I knew, and so did the others. However, it was funny when Nate and Pat met Andi.

"How old are you?" Nate asked her.

"Nathaniel!" Pat said.

"What? I'm curious." He shrugged.

"I'm seventeen," Andi said.

"Oh," they said. Nate and Pat glanced at each other.

"Is there a problem?" Jace asked them.

"No problem. Your uncle forgets he once robbed the cradle, too," Jonas said with a snicker.

Nate gave him a look. "Hey, I waited until she was eighteen."

"Well, that's what I'm doing," Jace said.

"I waited until she was eighteen to kiss her," Nate said.

"And tell my boy what happened after she turned eighteen." Jonas smirked.

"Nothing happened, nothing at all."

"Yeah, right. Nathaniel jumped on her," Cayson said while walking up.

"Cayson, shut up. You're not helping," Nate said.

"Nash got together with Maggie when she was seventeen," Jace told them.

"Leave me out of your reason," Nash said.

"I'm just saying, cuz," Jace said.

"Yeah, well, I hope you bought a big bottle of lotion because you'll need it," Nash said.

I couldn't help but laugh.

"Oh, haha. Yeah, wait until you need a bottle yourself, buddy," Jace said.

I swear those boys were something else. It was nice to see everyone. I wish it were under different circumstances than dealing with this mess.

If Lucille found out, everyone would be in trouble. We needed to hide it from her. That is easier said than done.

Nash pulled me to him as everyone looked on. He looked into my eyes, his steel grey meeting my blue ones. "I love you."

"I love you more."

"Mags, there's no one else for me. You're it."

I smiled as he kissed me while everyone looked on and smiled.

"They came a long way, didn't they?" Jonas asked Nate.

"We all have," Nate said. He looked at everyone who was standing there.

"Yeah, but it was worth it." Cayson smirked.

Nate and Jonas rolled their eyes. Leave it to one Gray boy to ruin a moment. Did I expect anything less? Nope, I didn't.

CHAPTER 17

THINGS TOOK AN INTERESTING TURN

After the parents' visit, they had left, but Andi stayed for a few days to visit Jace. They didn't have many chances to see each other. They made the most of her visit, with him bringing Andi home, so she wouldn't miss school. We would learn later what happened after Andi visited Jace.

Jaime and Bri went out for the evening, leaving them alone. While up in Jace's room, they made out until things took a turn between them. Things became heated between them as Andi helped Jace with his pants as he moved between her legs. Sliding her panties aside, he entered her, causing a gasp to release from her lips. His lips were against hers. Then he started moving inside of her, thrusting back and forth.

Both kept going, forgetting one crucial detail. It would cause a more significant issue than we knew.

Jace and Andi figured it was a moment of weakness between them. They decided to wait until she turned eighteen the next time it happened. It had been Andi's first time. Both realize they took a chance when they ended up having sex that night. The rest of the weekend, they hung out. They said no one had happened between them. He took her home with plans of one of them visiting soon. The problem is that their visit would happen sooner than expected.

The rest of us were dealing with the shenanigans of our own. Jace received a phone call from a hysterical Andi as he was meeting Jaime after class.

"Andi? Whoa, slow down. I can't understand you," he said as Jaime wondered what she was saying.

Jace tried to get Andi to explain things. Bri walked up to meet with Jaime.

"What's going on?" She asked Jaime.

"I don't know. Andi called Jace about something. Jace is trying to get her to calm down. He's trying to find out what's going on."

"What? Don't do anything. I'll be right there," he told her as he hung up.

Jaime and Bri looked at him as he looked back at them. "Is anyone up for a road trip?"

Jaime and Bri looked at each other. Whatever was going on with Andi wasn't good. Not if Jace was leaving school to see her.

Without telling the rest of us, the three set off to drive back home. Jace, Jaime, and Bri went to find out what the hell was going on. On the car ride back home, Jace filled in both on what was going on with Andi, stunning them.

"Are you freaking kidding me? Dad will kill you when he finds out," Jaime said as Jace drove.

"It's not like we meant for this to happen. It did," Jace said.

"How does one's dick land inside of a chick without a raincoat? Explained this to me because I'm dying to know," Jaime said.

"Christ, you sound like Nixon. It happened, okay?" Jace said.

Jaime looked at Bri. "See, it happened, no big deal."

"It's a big deal once my parents find out," She told him.

"Not if I can help it," Jace said as he picked up speed, driving to Andi's house. That was the one thing about Jace. He was all about doing the right thing. No matter how stupid of a decision he made. Trust me. This decision was foolish on his part.

They arrived at Andi and Bri's house, and Bri went to get Andi. The two of them later appeared from the house with the guise Bri had come home to see Andi since Andi was missing Bri. Their parents bought it. The Grays would have known something was up. The only time the brothers saw each other was when they were plotting something. It was a known fact.

The four of them drove to a secluded spot as Jace pulled in and parked the car. Jaime and Bri sat in the back seat. Andi sat in the front passenger seat while Jace sat on the driver's side, not saying a word.

"I know it was a shock. I thought you should know," Andi said as he sat there, not saying anything. "I'll understand if you don't want this. I'll manage by myself if I have to." She was letting Jace off the hook about the whole situation. Most guys would jump at the chance. Jace being Jace, decided he didn't want to be like most guys.

He turned to her. "Andi, you don't have to do this alone. I won't allow it. It isn't a situation you have to deal with alone. I have to deal with it, too."

"What about the school, Jace?" Jaime asked him.

Jace turned his head until he was facing Jaime. "I'll still finish school, but I'm responsible, too. It takes two to tango. Jaime, it wouldn't be right if I left Andi to fend for herself. What kind of guy would that make me?"

Jaime knew there was no arguing. No matter what they said, Jace would do the right thing.

A voice of reason spoke up. "It's admirable that Jace wants to do the right thing. However, I'm not sure how Mom and Dad will react to the news. Good luck, Andi."

Andi's face contorted in horror while Jace sighed as Jaime placed his palm on his face. No matter what they did, it wouldn't matter. It would be how Jace handles it that would make the difference.

He started the car and pulled out of the parking spot, driving with the others in the vehicle. Jace would do the right thing. It would surprise us with what was to follow. With Jonas and Karen, someone else would put things into perspective for them.

CHAPTER 18

TROUBLE WITH A CAPITAL T

We were in the school's hallway when Jace's phone went off. He looked at it and answered, "Andi?"

Get off me! He heard her scream.

"Andi!" He said into the phone.

I told you to stay out of things! He heard a deep voice say on the other end.

Jace put it on speaker, and we heard scuffling and banging. Nash and Jace looked at each other. Nash grabbed my hand as we ran to the car.

On our way to Andi, Nash called Nixon to fill him in on what was happening. Jace used the find my phone app to locate her. Nash sped towards Andi's school.

It took two hours, but he pulled up to the school, and the car screeched to a halt. Jace didn't waste any time getting out of the vehicle. Nash and I ran after him.

He busted through the doors and ran towards the signal, then found her. Two guys were attacking her. A fire burned in his eyes as he charged towards them, knocking them off their feet. "Get off her!"

Nash followed suit. They beat the shit out of the two guys while I tended to Andi. She was bleeding. I stayed with her while they finished off the two guys. Then Jace walked over, and I got out of the way. He lifted her bridal style and carried her out of the school.

"It's okay, baby. I've got you, and no one will ever hurt you again."

She buried her head into this chest as he carried her out to the car. She lifted her head. "You came."

"Always," he told her.

With that, she passed out.

We took her to the hospital to have her injuries treated. Jace stayed with her while we waited in the waiting room. Her parents showed up a few minutes later, frantic.

They talked to Nash, and he explained what happened, then made their way back to see their daughter.

"This seems familiar," I said to him, not realizing why.

He arched an eyebrow. "Yeah, it's too familiar."

*****

It was a while before Jace came out. When he appeared, he explained what was going on. "They're keeping her overnight for observation."

"How is she?" Nash asked him.

"Pretty beat up. Nash, those boys have been making her life a living hell. I want to kill them for hurting her."

"I know." Nash understood how he felt since it was the same way he thought about me.

We talked as her parents came out, stopping to speak to us. "Thank you. We had reservations about Andi dating someone much older, but not anymore," her dad said to Jace.

"With all due respect, sir, I love your daughter. I hate that I'm so far from her," he said.

"Jace, what are you saying?" Nash asked him.

He turned to Nash. "I'm taking Andi back with us."

"Oh, Hun, we can't let you do that," her mom said.

"I'm not backing down. Andi is my girl, and those animals went after her. I won't allow that to happen again."

We stood there. Jace was dead serious, and he would not back down with Andi.

Nash and I glanced at each other.

"What about school?" Her dad asked him.

"I can set up online courses for her. She can still graduate," Jace said.

"And where will she live?" Her mom asked him.

"With me," he said.

Nash and I looked at him with surprise.

"She's seventeen," her dad said.

What he said next shocked us. "Andi's my wife!"

Nash and I stood there with brows lifted and mouth agape.

"What?" Her dad asked as they stood there.

"Shit," he said.

"When did this happen?" Her parents asked.

Jace stood there, silent as Nash asked, "Jace?"

Jace leaned over and whispered something to him. Nash's expression changed to beyond shock. What in the world?

Nash leaned over, whispering something to me. My eyes widened since I wasn't expecting that news.

"Well," her father said.

"A few weeks ago, when Bri came down to visit her," Jace told him.

"That is impossible. Andi needs parental consent since she's a minor," her dad said.

"She doesn't need parental consent," Nash said.

"Like hell, she doesn't," he told Nash.

"Not when she's pregnant, she doesn't," Nash told him.

The pregnancy news shocked her parents. They looked at Jace. "Fine. She's all yours." Her dad stormed out with her mom.

Jace sat down and put his head in his hands.

"Jace, what were you thinking?" Nash asked him.

"Nash, it happened the night everyone came for a visit. I wanted to wait. She makes me feel things I have never felt. After that night, we promised to wait until she turned eighteen. Then one day, she called me hysterical. What was I supposed to do?"

"Um, well, wrapping it would have been an excellent start."

"Yeah, I know. Trust me. I know." Jace sighed.

"Who else knows?"

"Jaime and Bri. They went with us when I went to talk to her, then we eloped."

"So, I take it your mom and dad don't know?" I asked him.

"No, we would have told them. We were trying to find the right time." Jace sighed. He sat there, rubbing his face with his palms.

"Do you love her?" Nash asked him.

"What kind of question is that? Of course, I love her!"

"Hey, I'm asking because you had better hope that is enough when Uncle Jonas finds out," Nash said, reminding Jace of his dad's temper. Jonas was easygoing, but he had a temper like his brothers. He was a Gray boy.

"Shit."

The shit would hit the fan when Jonas and Karen found out what Jace had done. At least, he was responsible and married her. That was a plus.

*****

After they released Andi, we had to pay a visit to Jace's parents. Jace explained to Andi what happened with her parents. It upset her, but he assured her that he would take care of her.

We let them go in first to break the news, then waited. After ten minutes, we walked inside to hear yelling.

"What were you thinking?" Jonas asked him.

Yep, Jonas wasn't too happy.

"It was an accident, Dad!" Jace said.

"No, a car accident is an accident. This situation is not using your brain."

"We got caught up in the moment!"

"You still use your raincoat!"

"Like you did?" We heard someone ask.

We turned to see Nate standing there.

"Great, that's all I need. Why are you here?" He asked Nate.

"Nash called me." He shrugged.

"What's he talking about?" Jace asked Jonas.

"Nothing," Jonas said.

"Like hell, it's nothing. Your old man knocked up your mother and wasn't married," Nate said, throwing Jonas under the bus. Well, damn.

"Oh," Jace said, looking at Jonas with annoyance.

"Yeah, but I married your mom," Jonas said.

"Yeah, well, I married Andi," Jace said.

"What?" The three of them asked. Nash and I placed our faces in our palms.

"What do you mean you got married? She's seventeen and needs parental consent," Jonas told him.

"Not if the girl is pregnant," Jace told him.

Jonas turned and threw his arms up. "Fantastic!"

"Ma?" Jace asked, turning to his mom for help.

"Well, I guess there's no going back now." Karen winced as Jonas glared at her.

"I am so glad I'm not pregnant," I said in a low voice to Nash

They all looked at me as Nash placed his palm on his face.

"Too soon?" I asked him.

He looked at me and said, "A little."

*****

Jonas yelled as Andi cried. Jonas and Karen finally relented and welcomed Andi to the family. Jace took responsibility for Andi and brought her back with us.

He also signed her up for online classes, so she could finish high school. When he graduates, he will start working to support them.

I sat in the front with Nash as they sat in the back. I turned and saw them with each other. They held onto each other, and I realized Jace didn't marry her because she was pregnant. He did it because he loved her.

He wanted to sacrifice his future for her, but she wouldn't allow it. Who would have ever guessed that one night at a party would lead to this? Love comes from the most unexpected places.

We returned and dropped Jace and Andi off at his place; then we headed back to the house. As we got out of the car, I asked Nash, "Do you think they'll make it?"

Nash looked at me. "I know they will."

"What makes you so sure?"

He wrapped his arms around me. "Because we did."

With that, I smiled. Nash and I had a secret of our own, and only his brothers knew. What's our secret? Well, I guess you'll have to wait to see.

CHAPTER 19

OUR FIRST CHRISTMAS ENGAGED

Now that everyone knows about Jace and Andi. That was making the boys get the itch to settle down with their women. At one point, Nash was giving me a look, and I told him to back off. A baby could wait.

"Come on, Mags! By the time it gets here, we'll be married," he said.

"Nash, I get you to want a baby, but no. What is wrong with you, guys? Jace told everyone he and Andi got married and are expecting. It's like your brains went on vacation," I said across the bed.

"Ma said it's something about feeling the need to reproduce. It happened with her and Dad." he shrugged.

I shook my head. "Come on. We need to finish packing, so we can head home."

"Fine."

As we finished packing, we heard the girls yell at the brothers.

"Nixon, it's not happening!" Kat said.

"But come on, Kat! You enjoy hiding the sausage!" He spoke.

Ew, gross. Nobody wanted to know about Nixon's kinky side. I know I didn't.

"Not today, you horny bastard!"

"Nathan, I swear to god if you popped a hole in any of your raincoats. I'll beat you!" Macey told Nathan.

"Macey, I did no such thing! Well, at least, not yet," he said.

"No, Noah! It's a no!" Marcy told Noah.

"Marcy, *please!*" He spoke.

Nolan and Brook popped their heads into our bedroom. "You know, for me being the biggest horn dog there is, am I the only one who doesn't have the urge to procreate?"

I looked at Nash, annoyed as I said, "It seems so."

"What is with everyone?" Brook asked us. "It's like someone ends up pregnant, and everyone has some weird fetish to get pregnant."

"Not the girls, but the guys," I said.

"What?" He asked as he was packing.

"What about the others?" Nolan asked me.

"Well, Meg told Carson that she would cut off his balls. Gema told Caleb that he needs to get his head out of his ass. Bri told Jaime to run far and long. I don't think I want to know what she has planned," I said to them.

"The only one not thinking about kids beside us is Cody," Nolan told us.

"How's he doing?" Nash asked him.

"He pretty much goes to school and stays in his room. Carson and Caleb have tried to help him, but he doesn't want their help," Nolan said.

Cody was still nursing a broken heart and had distanced himself from everyone. My heart ached for him.

We finished packing and went downstairs, so we could head home. That should be a fun Christmas break. Wait until Grammy finds out about Jace and Andi. God help us all.

*****

We arrived home, and the girls went home to their families, leaving the boys grumpier than usual. They needed the space between them. The boys have lost their damn minds. I'm sure Jace didn't expect this to happen.

Christmas should be enjoyable with everyone coming, including Lucille and Grayson. Oh, did I forget to mention, no one told them the exciting news? No? Yeah, they don't know but are about to find out.

We got ready for Christmas like we usually do when we heard the doorbell. I walked over and answered it to find Lucille and Grayson standing there. They grabbed me and hugged me, causing my arms to flail.

"Oh, we missed you, Maggie," Grayson told me.

"I missed you, too, Grayson," I said, trying to catch my breath.

"Ma. Dad. Could you let Maggie go before you crush her?" Nate asked them while walking over to us.

"Nathaniel, it's been a while. Give us a break," Grayson said.

"Ma had seen Maggie," he said.

"Yeah, well, I love this girl. She reminds me of Patty. Where is my favorite daughter?" Grammy asked, waving Nate off.

"She's in the kitchen." He thumbed toward the kitchen.

She made her way to the kitchen as Grayson let go of me and looked at Nate. "What are you and your brothers hiding?"

"What makes you think we're hiding anything?" He asked, denying that they were hiding an enormous secret.

"Nathaniel, I know you and your brothers. You're always hiding something from us."

"We aren't hiding anything."

"That is fine. Keep telling yourself that. But your mother will sniff it out. She's like a dog with secrets." He walked past Nate. Nate looked at me, and I smiled.

*****

With Lucille and Grayson staying with us, we had to watch what we said. If we could keep them from finding out until after the wedding, that would be great.

Christmas arrived, and so did everyone else. Everyone was enjoying themselves except for Cody. I knew he was not himself, as did everyone else. So, I talked to him.

"Cody?" I said as I approached him.

He was standing off by himself, not interacting with anyone.

"Hey, Maggie."

"It's okay to feel bad."

"I wish I didn't feel bad all the time. It's like I can't breathe. It hurts so much."

"You loved her, didn't you?"

"Yeah, and I still do. I know people think it's stupid." He shook his head with the whole notion of loving someone like Becca.

"It's not stupid." I knew what it was like to like someone and realize the feeling wasn't mutual.

"I mean, most guys would move on, but I loved everything about her. Why couldn't she love me? Why did she want to cause trouble?"

They're the questions everyone asks themselves when a relationship doesn't work out.

"I don't think it was that simple."

"What do you mean?"

Ding dong.

"You should answer the door."

He set his drink down, then answered the door. He found Becca standing there.

"Becca?"

"Hi, Cody."

"What are you doing here?"

"I wanted to apologize to you and everyone else."

He looked at her with knitted brows.

"I was having issues, and I talked to my parents. They suggested I see my doctor. Cody, I have bipolar."

I glanced at everyone as their faces dropped.

"I know it's not an excuse, but they had to put me on medication. I'm sorry. I never meant to hurt you or anyone else. If you're angry with me, I understand," Becca said.

Nash leaned down. "You knew."

"I had a feeling. I've been talking to Becca," I said.

"And thus, I love you."

I smiled at him.

Cody pulled her to him. He kissed her and said, "I'm not angry. I was, but now I felt lost. I wanted you."

"And you are the only one I want."

"So, you don't have the hots for my cousin?"

"Oh, he's hot. But he's not my type."

"Thanks," Nash said with an offended look, and I smacked him.

"My type is the person who loves Harry Potter as much as I do." She smiled at Cody.

"Yep, that isn't me," Nash said as I giggled.

Cody smiled and kissed her again. At least, someone got a happy ending.

Then Grammy turned to us. "Okay, who's pregnant?"

Our eyes widened.

"Don't act so surprised. I can smell the hormones a mile away," Grammy told us.

Well, damn.

We stood there as she sized up each girl with a 'nope' response while moving to the next girl. Then she zeroed in on Jace and Andi. The next thing we knew, she smacked him upside the head.

"Ow! Grammy!" He rubbed his head.

"Boy, what is wrong with you? You never forget your raincoat," she told him as she glared at him. Andi moved behind him. "Oh, sweetie, I don't think you're immune. Get your ass over here."

Andi moved back, and Grammy smacked her upside the head.

"Grammy!" Jace said.

"Hush, child."

Jace shut up.

"Now that we got that out of the way, what were you two thinking?"

"Well......"

"Jason, she's seventeen and still in high school. By doing such a stupid thing, you took her youth from her. Was it worth it?"

We stared at him.

Jace looked at Andi as he said, "Yes."

We watched them.

"She's amazing."

Andi smiled.

He turned back to Lucille. "And that's why I married her."

She studied them and crossed her arms. "Is that so?"

"Yeah."

"Well, well, well." She tapped her fingertips on her arms and her foot on the floor. "At least, you did the right thing."

Our jaws dropped.

"Now, I want to know what you intend to do with her education."

"She is taking online courses to finish high school. Then she will take college classes. I've talked to someone, and I have a job lined up when I graduate. It will allow us to live close to the school, so she can get her degree." He wrapped his arms around Andi and held her tight.

"I see."

We weren't sure what to think at this moment. Oh, boy. Here comes the hammer.

"At least, you weren't a complete dumb ass in all this." And there it was. She turned to Andi. "Well, I guess I can welcome you to the family. You seem like a sweet girl. How the hell you ended up with the likes of him is beyond me?" She pointed at Jace.

He gave Grammy an annoyed look as Andi said, "Funny thing. I pursued him."

Lucille arched an eyebrow, then her lips formed into a smirk. "Good girl, because Jason is one of the unusual ones. He's like his daddy."

"I'm confused."

Lucille took her hand. "I might be hard on my boys and grandsons, but they're everything to me. I want them to be happy. Jason deserves to be happy, and if you make him happy, then so be it. I know he'll take excellent care of you, or he'll deal with me." She gave Andi a wink and a smile.

"Now, let's eat." Grammy went back into the kitchen.

"What happened?" Andi asked us.

"You got Grammy's approval," I said with a grin.

"Oh."

We looked at her until she realized what that meant.

"Oh!"

"Come on, Wifey. Let's go feed, junior," Jace said, taking her hand and leading her to the table. Everyone else followed suit.

I headed towards the kitchen when Nash stopped me. "You know, I was thinking. We should wait."

"Oh? And why do you say that?"

"Because one secret is enough for us. Plus, I don't want to get smacked by Grammy anytime soon."

"Well, not until she finds out." I giggled.

He gave me a look and chased after me into the kitchen. It seems a Gray grandson wasn't only married but having a baby, which meant more were on the way.

They say happiness comes from the most unexpected places, but love is so much more. The Grays might be crazy, but with the family, they love deeply and fiercely. If you get a chance to be a part of it, you're lucky.

We were heading towards more craziness as the wedding drew closer for us. It wouldn't be the Gray family if there weren't some craziness.

CHAPTER 20

THE BROTHERS ARE AT IT AGAIN

After Christmas, you would think things would calm down and become somewhat routine. Nope, not even close. The brothers and cousins had a little fun at our expense. I swear they want to die a painful death.

"You know the girls will kill us," Noah told them.

"Eh, they won't do shit," Nixon said as they walked up to our rooms carrying buckets.

"They need to lighten up. The girls have been so damn touchy lately," Nathan said.

"Did they forget who they're dating?" Nolan asked him.

"Yep," Nathan said.

All five doors flung open, and so did the water in the buckets of ice water.

"Nash!" I said, startled from my sleep to an ice-cold bath.

"Oops, my bad." He chuckled.

"I'll chop off your balls, Nixon!" Kat said.

"Yeah, but you must catch me first!" He spoke.

"So, not funny, Nathan!" Macey said.

"Wet tee shirts are always fun." He laughed.

"Noah, you're a dead man!" Marcy said.

"But a happy dead man," he said.

"Nolan, you twerp!" Brook said.

"Bite me. Bite me a lot," Nolan told Brook while wiggling his eyebrows at her.

We scrambled out of bed and chased after them. The boys ran, we tackled them, and they pinned us down—those damn Gray brothers.

Then things took a turn as they picked us up and carried us to the bedrooms. They're such horny bastards.

If Nash and I kept this up, we would be the next couple expecting a little bundle of joy.

He rolled off me as we caught our breaths.

"Haven't you ever heard of a good morning kiss?" I asked him.

He grinned. "And what fun would that be?"

I pulled the blankets over me and cuddled up next to him. He wrapped his arms around me.

"You know this means war?" I told him.

"Pretty much." He smirked.

I laughed.

*****

And war it was. We went all out with the pranks. They ranged from someone getting pudding in their bra to hot sauce in their boxers. Let's not forget the shaving cream and cheese. Thank you, demon spawn, for your suggestion.

If it was one thing I learned about the brothers, you must fight fire with fire, well, almost. Someone got their head shaved as another got their brows cut. A third got their legs shaved, and the fourth got their armpits shaved. Finally, someone got their nether regions shaved. Who may you ask? You're about to find out.

"You know they'll kill us," Marcy told us.

"Yeah, but they're lucky considering the shit they pulled on me through the years," I said to her.

We all held electric razors in our hands.

"How long before they wake up?" Kat asked us.

"Well, the sleeping pills should wear off in about a minute," Marcy said.

"I like this family." Brook grinned.

We stood there and waited, then we heard it. "What the…"

"You've got to be kidding me!" Another one said.

"This is horseshit!" A third one said.

"For the love of god!" A fourth yell came.

"Oh, my god! It itches!" That was the last one.

10, 9, 8, 7, 6, 5, 4, 3, 2, and…….

All five doors opened. We stood there, trying to stifle a laugh.

"Mags! That is so not funny! Grammy will kill me!" Yep, I shaved Nash's head.

"At least, it wasn't your brows," I said.

We looked at Nixon without brows. Yeah, he was fuming.

"Marcy," Noah spoke through gritted teeth as he glared at her.

"Yes, honey?" She asked.

"Was it necessary to shave my pits?" He asked her.

"Well, no, but it was funny." She giggled.

"At least, she shaved your pits. I got my legs shaved," Nathan said, yanking up his sweatpants leg. He glared at Macey.

"Well, I'm sure you would look great in a dress with those killer legs." She snickered.

"I don't know why you four are complaining. This shit itches," Nolan said as he kept itching his crotch.

Nash walked over to me as I stood there and said, "You have learned well, grasshopper."

"Thank you, master. I have learned from the best," I said to him.

"Now, with your glorious achievement comes a large reward."

"Oh yeah, and what may that be?" I asked with a side glance.

Nash looked at his brothers, and a smirk formed upon their faces. Well, shit.

*****

Okay, here is the thing about messing with a Gray brother, prepared to deal with the consequences of your actions. Because they always one-up you.

"Nash, this is not funny!" I spoke.

"Well, you shouldn't have shaved my head," he said.

"Nixon!" Kat said.

"Nah, uh, Katrina, you deserve this for lack of eyebrows." He pointed to the fake eyebrows Nolan drew on his face.

"Hunny," Marcy said to Noah.

"Forget it, Marcy. Your charms won't get you out of this one," Noah told her.

"Nathan, you are so not getting sex for a month," Macey told Nathan.

"I can live with that. Hello, Rosie," he said while raising his hand and wiggling his fingers.

"Nolan, I'm so going to beat you!" Brook told him.

"Sure, sure, excuse me while I itch myself to death," he said as he itched his crotch.

We heard voices.

"And that's our cue," Nash told them.

They walked away, leaving us in the middle of the school tied up to two poles in our underwear.

"Nashville!" I spoke.

"Bye." He walked away while waving me off.

People stopped and started laughing as we squirmed, trying to get out of the ropes they had used to tie us to two poles.

Marco, Jasper, and Paul walked up.

"Do we even want to know?" Jasper asked me.

"Yeah, never mess with a Gray brother," I said.

They shrugged and started to untie me when Nixon said, "Untie them, and you're next!"

They removed their hands and held them up in defense.

"Marco!" I said to my brother.

"Sorry, sis, but a brother has to stick together with a brother," he told me.

Then the cousins walked up with their girls and started laughing at us.

"This is so not funny!" Kat told them.

"Hey, we're the demon spawn, but with the Gray Brothers, even we can't match them." Cody laughed.

We sighed. Great.

We stayed where we were most of the day, all thanks to getting tied up. People walked past us, pointed, and laughed. So, we had to suck it up.

After the last class ended for the day, we heard someone ask, "Did you learn your lesson?"

We looked at the brothers, and I sighed. "Yeah."

"Good," Nash told me.

They walked over and untied us, then handed our clothes to us. We pulled them on. They went to hug us as we pushed them away, running to the bathroom. Eight hours is a long time not to pee. My bladder wanted to explode.

As we finished up, I walked out of the stall and washed my hands along with Kat, Marcy, and Brook. We heard someone heave. We stopped, turned off the water, and looked at each other. The only one missing was Macey, who was tossing her cookies in one stall.

I looked at the girls as they looked at me. We sighed. She came out of the stall and saw us looking at her. "What?" She walked over to the sink and started washing her hands.

"Are you okay, Macey?" I asked her.

"Yeah, I'm fine. It's something I ate," Macey said.

"Are you sure, Mace?" Kat asked.

"I'm fine. Why are you looking at me like that?" She asked us.

"Because we haven't eaten anything in eight hours," Brook said.

She started fidgeting and wouldn't look at us.

"Macey, how long?" I asked her.

She looked at me. "I don't know what you're talking about."

"Macey?" Marcy made eye contact with her twin.

She closed her eyes, and we sighed.

"Macey, it's okay," I said.

"Maggie, you don't understand," she said.

"What don't I understand?"

"I can't do this alone!" She said as we stood there, confused.

"What are you talking about?" Marcy asked her.

"Nathan still has another year of school left after we finish. I'll be all alone in this," she said.

"Who says?" Kat asked her.

"I can't make him give up on school. It's not right," Macey told Kat.

"Then you need to talk to him. It takes two to tango," Brook told her.

"I can't. Please promise me you won't say anything," Macey said as tears fell down her cheeks.

We looked at her. That was easier said than done. There's no way we could keep this from the brothers, especially Nathan. But like the fools we are, we agreed. Remind me why this idea was superb?

We came out of the bathroom, and everyone walked away as Nash looked at me. "Is everything okay?"

I looked at him, and he looked at me.

"Do I even want to know?" He asked me.

"I don't think so."

"Mags?"

"Nash, the shit is about to hit the fan."

His eyes widened. He watched his brothers and the girls walk away. Then he turned back to me. "Well, shit."

Yep, things took another turn for us.

CHAPTER 21

BABY LOVE, MY BABY LOVE: A VALENTINE'S DAY CHAPTER

Valentine's Day is a day of love and romance. Well, unless you're a Gray brother. It's a day filled with chaos and yelling, which brings us to our present situation and brings us a visit from Nate and Pat.

The day started okay. We were planning on spending the day doing romantic things. Someone opened their mouth. By someone, I mean Nolan.

The twins were talking when Nolan walked up and asked, "So, how do you think Ma and Dad take the news, Nathan?"

"What news?" Nathan asked.

Nolan looked at him as Nathan looked confused and said, "Never mind." He turned to leave, and Nathan grabbed him.

"Listen, you freaky tool. You had better start talking, or you can forget getting romantic with Brooky poo," Nathan said.

"It's nothing," Nolan said.

"Nolan," Noah said.

"Nash and Maggie were talking about Macey knocked up." He shrugged.

"What?" The twins asked as Nixon walked by them, stopping and turning around. "Ma and Dad will kill you, junior."

The twins bolted upstairs. Then the yelling started.

Nash and I came out of our bedroom to find Nixon and Nolan listening at Nathan's door.

"What's with all the yelling?" Nash asked them.

"Asked the procreation team in there," Nixon said while pointing at Nathan's door.

Nash and I looked at each other with wide eyes as we listened at the door.

Then the door whipped open as Nathan said, "It's so nice to know my damn brothers knew before me!"

"They didn't know at first!" Macey told him.

"Oh yeah, then who?"

"The girls did!"

My eyes widened as my mouth went agape.

"What?" He asked.

Nathan came out and shot me a glare before storming past us. Yep, Nathan was not happy.

Noah came out of the bedroom while on the phone.

"Who are you calling?" Nash asked him.

"Who else? Ma and Dad," Noah told him.

The boys looked at each other, then at Noah, and tackled him for his phone. While struggling for the phone, the line connected, and someone let it slip. "You can't tell them about Macey being pregnant," Nixon said.

She's what? A deep voice asked.

They all stopped and stayed silent.

I know you're there. I can hear you breathing and plotting. Your mother and I'll be there shortly. Run, and I'll chop off your balls. We heard Nate say on the other end.

Click!

Well, that went better than expected. The boys couldn't leave. They sent their cousins to find Nathan and drag his ass back to the house to face their parents.

Nathan returned with Jace and Jaime. He found his parents standing there, along with his brothers and the girls. He walked over to his dad.

"So, would you like to explain to me why you ran out on your girl when she needs you?" Nate asked Nathan.

"Nope," Nathan said to Nate, not wanting to discuss it.

That was all it took. Nate hauled off and punched Nathan in the mouth, causing Nathan to fly backward and us to gasp in shock.

"Nathaniel!" Pat said.

"Patricia, I'm sick of his attitude. He's a grown-ass man. He's twenty years old and acts like he is two," he told her. I had never seen Nate raise his voice to Pat before or strike one of their boys. That shocked the hell out of me.

"Well, you're acting like a five-year-old," she said, helping Nathan up.

Nathan dusted himself off. "So, my anger doesn't matter, only when everyone else is."

"That's not true, honey," Pat told him.

"Are you sure? Because I'm sure, it is. I didn't see Dad strike anyone else when they screwed up, yet I'm the one that gets the hit," he said as his bottom lip quivered.

"Nathan," Pat said.

"I'm angry, Ma. I'm angry that my girl couldn't tell me before everyone else knew," he said as he cried. She wrapped her arms around him, holding his head while she rubbed his back, offering comfort.

"So, you're not angry that Macey is pregnant?" She asked him.

"No, I'm happy, but those tools knew before me," he said as he pointed at his brothers, who looked around and whistled.

She looked at Nate, who sighed. Macey walked over, and Pat handed Nathan off to her. She comforted him as Pat walked over to Nate. "Now, don't you feel like a horse's ass."

He gave her an unamused look. "Patty, we still have the matter of dealing with him having one more year of school. She's graduating, and they're not married."

She looked at everyone, then smiled. "Then, I guess today would be the perfect day for a wedding."

We all looked at each other. I guess another Gray boy was getting married.

*****

Okay, so Valentine's Day is a joyful day with love and laughter. People celebrate love and happiness. We celebrate a wedding. The only problem was trying to find a minister on short notice.

Today every minister is booked. That is fantastic. What's a Gray to do? But go online and become an ordained minister, as Nixon did. Don't ask.

He had to answer a bunch of questions, and poof, he became a minister. Since they had to wait until tomorrow to get the marriage license, they had the ceremony. Then they'll make it legal. There's nothing like doing things half-ass-backward.

"I need a book," Nixon said.

"What kind of book?" Noah asked him.

"I don't care. I need a book."

"Why?"

"Because all ministers hold a book. I need to look proper."

"Yeah, but they hold a Bible," Nash said.

"Bible, book, it's all the same thing." Nixon waved his hand around.

"Since when?" Nash asked him.

"Uh, since I became a minister, and you may call me Father Nixon."

"That's a priest, you tool, and you're not my father," Nash told him.

"Well, our father is Rocky Balboa. I'm much nicer," Nixon said.

"Since when?" Nathan asked him.

"Since forever, you twit," he said.

"You're a minister. No name-calling," Nolan told him.

"Pft, I'm the minister who will give you a fat lip if you don't shut your trap," Nixon told him.

Geez, Nixon was a scary minister and not helpful.

I leaned over to Nash. "Please tell me he's not marrying us."

"Nope, he's the best man," he told me.

"Oh, God," I said.

"Nope, you'll scream that later." He smirked.

I placed my palm on my face.

"Can we get on with this before I'm too old to give a shit?" Nate asked us.

"You're already old, but that's beside the point," Nixon said.

"Nix," Nate said, giving him a look.

"Yeah?" He smiled.

"Nathan won't be the only one getting my fist," Nate said, holding up his fist as Nixon's eyes widened.

We all looked at Nate as Nixon said, "Dearly beloved, I gather us today to join these two idiots in holy matrimony. My tool brother doesn't know how to wear a raincoat. It's that, or he put a pinhole in it as he planned to do."

We all looked at Nathan, who looked around whistling.

"Lord, we're joining frick and frack in holy matrimony. We hope and pray they don't screw up their seed, who might be my niece or nephew. I'm hoping for a nephew. Girls aren't fun."

"Nixon!" Kat said.

"Well, except for my baby." He winked.

"Junior, do you take one of the double mint twins as your wife?"

Nathan rolled his eyes at him. "Yes."

"And double mint twin, do you take numbnuts here as your husband?" He asked Macey.

She arched an eyebrow at him. "Yes."

"Cool, at least, we know you both agree," he said as Nate was growing irritated, and we were trying not to laugh.

"Nixon!" Nate said.

"Shush, old man. We're having a wedding, and you're interrupting. That reminds me. Does anyone object to this unholy union? Man, they have been unholy." He glanced around. "No? Good, because that would suck. Back to the fact you both agreed to be bound to each other for the rest of your lives. The only way of getting out of this is death," he told them.

"Is your brother on something?" Jace asked Nash.

"Nope, that is Nixon being Nixon."

"I'm so glad he didn't marry Andi and me."

"That reminds me. Did the ban get lifted?"

"Dude, the ban got lifted the minute we got back to the house. My wife's hormones are nuts." He sighed.

"Glad you got over that hang-up." Nash smirked.

"Hey, peanut gallery. Do you want to discuss Jace's sex life later? We're having a wedding," Nixon told them. They shrugged as Nixon finished. "With the power invested in me, I pronounce you, the Devil and Mrs. Devil, themselves."

Nathan and Macey stared at him.

"Don't look at me. Kiss each other, you damn fools," Nixon said.

Nathan turned and kissed Macey.

"I could do something like that. That was fun." Nixon smirked. Oh, God. Heaven helps us if he becomes a minister.

"Well, that was something," Noah said.

"I thought it was great." Marcy giggled.

He glanced at her.

"Hunny, we should have Nixon do our wedding," she said to him.

"That would be a big fat no," Noah told her as he walked away from her.

"Oh, come on! At least, no one would fall asleep!" She spoke.

Marcy ran after Noah, trying to persuade him to have Nixon perform their wedding when they got married. Nash and I talked to Nathan and Macey.

"Well, it looks like you're the first one out of our family to marry," Nash said to him.

"And to have a kid," Nathan said to him.

"So, now what?" I asked him.

"Funny thing. I took some online courses over the summer for a few years. I get to graduate with the rest of you this spring," Nathan said to Nash.

Macey looked at him. "Are you serious?"

"Yeah, I wanted to surprise you. I have a job lined up. Our little papoose decided they had other plans," he said, placing his hand on her stomach.

"That reminds me. What did Nixon mean by putting holes in the raincoats?" I asked him.

"Oh, hey, Dad. Do you need some help?" He turned and walked over to his parents.

Macey looked at us. "I'm going to kill him."

We smiled.

Our senior year was ending as the wedding was getting closer. People started acting nuttier like the Grays. Noah also took summer online courses to graduate with us. Those two are two peas in a pod.

Did I mention Nixon is becoming a minister? His explanation was, he wanted to shake things up. Please do not let him be the guy who gets crazy with religion. Considering who this family is.

Things were getting started with everyone. Plus, Nash and I had a secret we were keeping, and only the brothers knew. That would be the best-kept secret yet.

CHAPTER 22

YOU'RE NUTS

With Nathan married and expecting a little one on the way, things had settled down, well, sort of. With March here, so was spring, and so were more surprises. What surprises, might you ask? I'm glad you asked because this one came from Carson and Meg.

We were all hanging out when both came in and said, "We got married!"

"Is she knocked up?" Nixon asked him.

"What? No," Carson said as he rolled his eyes.

"So, tell us again why you got married," Nash said as he shuffled the cards.

"Why not? I figured we would get married. Might as well do it now," he said.

"Wait until Aunt Dom finds out," Noah said.

"I'm not afraid of my mother," he said.

"Oh," Nathan said as he pulled out his phone and made a call.

"What's he doing? What are you doing?" Carson asked.

"Hello, Aunt Dominique. I'm calling to tell you Carson got married. Yep, I sure will. Here it's for you," he said, handing the phone to Carson.

Carson shot him a look and snatched the phone from him. "Hey, Momma," he said to his mother.

Do I sound like your mother? No! What the hell is wrong with you? Have you lost your damn mind? Cayson yelled on the other end.

"Hey, Dad." He sighed.

Don't hey, Dad, me. Is she pregnant?

"No," Carson said.

Then why would you get married now? I swear your mother dropped you on your head as a baby. And another thing, we'll have a serious talk when you come home. Tell your brothers that it includes them, you...

Man, Cayson has some colorful language, and he wasn't even on speakerphone.

Carson hung up and handed the phone back to Nathan. "You had to call my dad."

"Well, you're a dumb ass. So, yeah." Nathan shrugged.

"What's wrong with getting married?" He asked him.

"How about you aren't out of school, you don't have a job yet, and you didn't let me perform your ceremony? Forgive them, father, for being complete twits. Amen," Nixon said.

I couldn't help but snicker, as did Nash. Then Cody and Caleb walked in with their girls and started yelling at Carson.

"What the hell is wrong with you? You got married!" Caleb said.

"Yeah, so?" He shrugged.

"So, idiot, Momma will roast your nuts. It gives a whole new meaning to chestnuts roasting on an open fire," Cody said.

"Leave my nuts out of this," he said to them.

"It doesn't matter. It's not like you have any when your ma gets a hold of you," Nixon said.

Nash and I roared with laughter.

"What's so funny?" Carson looked at us.

"When Grammy finds out, you and Nathan had better run." He smirked.

"Well, shit," Nathan and Carson said.

"It's a wonderful thing that you're letting Grammy throw your wedding. By the time your wedding rolls around, everyone will be married," Noah told Nash.

As they all talked, my phone rang. Why was Kate calling me? I didn't have to work today.

"Hello?"

Maggie, can you come down to the bakery? I have something I would like to discuss with you and bring your fiancé. It involves him, too.

"Okay."

Click

"What was that about?" Nash asked me.

"Kate wants us to come to the bakery. She has a surprise for us," I told him.

He got up and grabbed my hand, leading me out of the house.

"Nash!"

"It could be important, woman!"

Well, okay, then.

*****

We made our way to the bakery and walked in to find Kate with some guy. He was an older gentleman with jet black hair and blue eyes. They looked related to each other.

"There she is," Kate said, walking from behind the counter and over to me. She hugged me, then hugged Nash. "Mason, this is Maggie and her fiancé, Nash Gray."

"Gray? Any relation to Grayson Gray?" He asked us.

"He's my granddad," Nash told him.

"He's an interesting man. I have done business with him a few times. Straight shooter," the man told Nash.

"Yeah, I don't think we came here to discuss my granddad."

"No, we had you come here because of a different reason," Kate said. "Follow me." She waved for us to follow her. We walked around the counter, and there were building plans.

"What's this?" I asked them.

"This, my dear, is an opportunity for both of you," she said.

Nash and I glanced at each other.

"Since you have been learning during your internship, we would like to help you expand on your creativity," she said.

"What did you have in mind?" Nash asked her.

"How would you both like your very own bakery after you graduate?" She asked.

Nash and I looked at each other, stunned.

*****

After talking to Kate and her older brother, Mason, they went over details with us.

"I don't know. I mean, it sounds great, but what's the catch?" Nash asked them, leaning with his back against the counter and his arms crossed.

"There's no catch. Kate figured it would give you two a head start, and you could make something out of it. I would offer financial backing. You can pay me back. Then the bakery is yours," Mason said.

"I want to discuss it with my dad first. I mean, it sounds like a great offer, but I'm not sure about it," he told Mason.

"What do you think, Maggie?" Kate asked me.

I looked at Nash, then at them. "We won't need to talk to Nate about it."

"Mags!" Nash said.

I gave him a look, then said, "Because as great as the offer sounds, if we do something like this, we want to do it together. Nash and I are in this together. If we fail, we fail together. If we succeed, we succeed together. Thanks, Kate, but I have to decline kindly."

Mason and Kate looked at each other then she smiled at me. "Very well, dear. At least, you know what you want. I admire your tenacity."

I smiled as Nash took my hand and led me out of the bakery. Once we were outside and out of earshot, he asked, "Why did you say no?"

"As the saying goes, if something is too good to be true, it usually is." It was true. No offer came without strings attached, no matter what you thought. If someone offered you something without strings, ask yourself why. It was a question I never wanted to ask.

He wrapped his arms around me. "And thus, I love you."

"I love you more." I wrapped my arms around his neck and kissed him.

Nash and I didn't want to take the easy road because we never have. We had our difficulties, but we always got through them together.

As we made our way back to the house, he stopped. "What?"

I had that look.

"Do you want to open a bakery?"

"Well, I love to bake, and you love to be creative. I figure we could do this together."

"And what would we call it?"

I gave it some thought. "How about The Gray Brother's Bakery?"

He looked at me.

"Thanks to you and your brothers, I got to learn more about life than I ever imagined. Plus, it wouldn't be dull." I grinned.

"No, I don't think it will be. I like it. I'll talk to Dad about it."

When he mentioned our idea, we would get a lot of support and help with it. Who wouldn't want to visit the Gray Brother's Bakery? I know I would.

CHAPTER 23

SOMETIMES, YOU NEED TO DANCE WHEN NO ONE IS LOOKING

Nash called Nate and explained to him what happened with the bakery idea. Nate agreed with our decision and offered to help us, as did Pat. It relieved me.

I didn't feel comfortable taking a chance with someone I didn't know. I know Kate's heart was in the right place, but something felt off. Opening a business is always a gamble.

Nash and I took a brief break with no one home and danced around the living room. We were getting so into it that we didn't hear people come in. "You two look like you're seizing out. Is there a reason you look like someone who got off crack?" Nixon asked us.

"Shut up. We're having fun," Nash said as he flipped me.

I landed on my wrist.

"Man down. Or should I say woman down? How about monkey down?" Nixon asked Kat as she rolled her eyes at him, then smacking him.

I grabbed my wrist in pain and let out a yelp.

"Shit," Nash said as he helped me up while I held my wrist.

"Good going, Tarzan. She should look adorable in a cast on your wedding day," Nixon said.

"Will you stop making snarky remarks and help me?" Nash asked him.

"What fun would that be?" Nixon shrugged.

Kat hauled off and smacked Nixon again.

"Fine, come on, Jane. Let's see if my twit of a brother broke your damn wrist," he said. He and Nash helped me to the car with Kat following behind us.

*****

The technician took me back and x-rayed my wrist. Afterward, I had to wait for the doctor to look at the x-ray.

"So, should you call Ma and Dad, or should I?" Nixon asked Nash.

"Why don't we wait until the doctor returns?" Nash asked.

I sat there, not caring since the pain meds kicked in and I was feeling no pain. The doctor walked in and looked at the x-ray. "From the looks of it, she has two minor fractures. It's a clean break, so a cast should work," the doctor said.

"Great." Nash sighed.

"She needs to return in a few days for her cast. We must wait for the swelling to go down. So, would you care to explain how she broke her wrist in two places?" the doctor asked them.

"Well, genius here decided that he wanted to spice things up in the bedroom if you know what I mean," Nixon said to the doctor.

"Nix!" Nash said.

"Hey, when you do the horizontal mambo, you need to leave the ceiling fan out of it," he said.

Nash shot him a glare, then turned to the doctor. "We were dancing in the living room. I flipped her, and she landed on her wrist," he said to the doctor, explaining how I got hurt.

"Oh, sure. Nash flipped her all right. He flipped her here and there if you get what I mean." Nixon smirked.

Nash was getting pissed by the minute.

"Make sure she takes it easy and takes her meds," the doctor said.

"Yeah, sure, Doc. Because we love listening to Elmer Fudd over here." Nixon thumbed at me.

The doctor gave him a strange look, then walked away.

They helped me up. "Was that necessary?" Nash asked him.

"No, but it was hella funny. The dude needs to lighten up." Nixon chuckled.

"Nix, he's a doctor. It's his job to be serious."

"And I'm the freaking pope. Although, the way I'm going, I'll become the next pope." Nixon smirked.

"How's they even possible? You need theology courses even to be a minister. The last time I checked, you didn't take any."

"Oh?"

"Yes."

"Did I forget to tell you? While in rehab, trying to figure out my life's purpose and understand my alcoholism, I switched majors."

Nash looked at him, a little confused. That made me a lot confused.

"No? Oh, yeah. I'm a minister and all that jazz." Nixon did jazz hands.

"Then what was with getting ordained and everything?"

"Well, I'm not a minister yet. I still must work with another minister as an associate minister. It's before they release me to the wild of my congregation. Because let me tell you, many people need Jesus. They're heathens." He smirked.

"Great. I don't want you to come over ranting and raving about how we need the Lord."

"Dude, you'll need the Lord when Ma and Dad find out what you did to Maggie. You better hope Jesus can save your ass because I'm sure hell hath no fury like Ma and Dad pissed off."

They took me to the house and called Nate and Pat to let them know what happened. I sat on the couch in a daze as they made the call, putting them on speaker.

Hello? I heard Nate's voice on the other end.

"Hey, Dad," Nash said.

Nash? What's going on?

"Oh, it's nothing much. I'm checking on wedding preparations."

What happened?

"What makes you think anything happened?" Nash tried to hide that I had broken my wrist.

Because you avoid wedding talk at all costs, when you're this happy, it means you did something stupid. Now, what did you do?

"Can't a son call his father to say hi?" Nash tried to avoid the obvious question.

There was silence as Nixon placed his palm on his face.

No. Now, what happened?

Then Nixon hijacked the conversation. "Well, you see, big brother threw Maggie around and fractured her wrist."

What? Nate asked.

"Well, they were dancing, and he flipped her. However, I told him to leave the ceiling fan out of it. But did he listen? No, he didn't."

Are you freaking serious?

"Okay, so it didn't involve a ceiling fan, but if they kept dancing to the bedroom, we wouldn't be in this mess. But then again, you never know." Nixon tried to be helpful, throwing us under the bus.

Nixon?

"Yeah?"

Shut up! And Nash?

I sat on the couch, loopy.

"Yeah, Dad?"

You better pray the cast comes off by your wedding, or you can deal with your mother and grandmother.

Click!

They looked at each other as Nixon said, "That went better than I thought it would."

Nash rolled his eyes and shook his head. The pain meds made me a drooling mess. Nash lifted and carried me to the bedroom since I was all doped up. Walking up the stairs would be a big fat no.

*****

I finally woke up, and my wrist was throbbing. I looked to see a soft cast on it and knew it meant one thing. I broke it. Great.

I smacked Nash with my pillow, startling him. "What the hell, Mags?"

I held up my arm and glared at him.

"Oh." He cringed.

"Oh? Nash, my wrist is broken! And all you can say is oh?" I gave him a skeptical look.

"My bad?" He shrugged.

I hit him again.

"Well, if it makes you feel better, if you don't have your cast off by the wedding, I'm a dead man."

I thought about it. "Yeah, that makes me feel better." I grinned.

He sighed, shaking his head. "Mags, I am sorry."

"Let's hope when we have our first dance, you don't flip me."

"Duly noted."

He placed his hand on my cheek as he pulled me into a kiss. We laid down, and I cuddled up next to him, being careful with my wrist. Until I got the hard cast, I had to be careful. It would be easier said than done.

*****

A few days later, Nash took me to get a cast for my wrist. I chose a neon purple cast. I wasn't a pink girl. Once they set it, Nash looked at the nurse and asked, "Do you have a black sharpie?"

"Yeah, why?" The nurse asked him.

"Because I need it."

The nurse shrugged and went to get a sharpie, returning with it and handing it to Nash. He took it and wrote something on my cast. Once he finished, he handed it back to the nurse.

I looked to read:

Watching for Comets

I smiled. It reminded me that Nash lost me once but found me again as I did with myself. It was also the song we picked for our first dance.

The song fits us.

CHAPTER 24

SEA CRUISE: A SPRING BREAK CHAPTER

For spring break, we all went on a sea cruise. Plus, this was our last hurrah with everyone before school ended, and Nash and I had our wedding. For our honeymoon, he had something special planned for us.

I wanted to relax. Since I had a cast, it limited me to what I could do. Kat hung with me along with Nash and Nixon. Nash still felt guilty. Good.

We settled into our rooms and met up with everyone on deck. Andi and Macey were leaning over the railing, heaving.

"Are they going to be, okay?" I asked Jace and Nathan.

"Yeah, let's give them a few minutes," Jace said.

"Shouldn't you be taking care of them? Some husbands you are," Nixon said.

They looked at each other, then walked over to their wives. I had to agree with Nixon. They could make sure the girls were okay.

"So, what's on the agenda?" Nolan asked us.

"We do our own thing and meet up for dinner," Nash said.

"Cool. Later," Nolan said as he and Brook walked away.

"You know we'll never see them the rest of the trip, right?" Noah asked us.

"As long as he isn't getting me arrested, I'm good." Nixon shrugged.

Everyone else split up and did their own thing while Nathan and Jace took care of their wives. I found a chaise lounge and sat down along with Kat. A deckhand brought over fruity drinks to us, and we took them.

Nash and Nixon checked out the boat.

"So, how do you feel about Nixon being a minister?" I asked Kat.

"You know, as weird as it sounds, I kind of like him being one. At least, he'll keep people entertained." She giggled.

I couldn't help but laugh.

As we talked, Nash and Nixon made their way back to us.

"Ladies, well, at least, one of you are," Nixon said to me with a smirk.

I rolled my eyes at him. They sat down, joining us. Before we knew it, Caleb and Gema came running towards us.

"Nixon," Caleb said as they came closer.

"Caleb, Nash, Kat, and Maggie. Now, we're all acquainted," Nixon said.

"Come on, Nixon. We need your help," Caleb said to him.

"Oh, fine. What do you need?" He asked.

"We need you to marry us," Caleb said.

Gema nodded while grinning.

"And pray tell, why?" Nixon gave him a sideways glance while the rest of us looked at each other.

"Well, um, you see......." Caleb rubbed the back of his neck with his palm.

We all looked at them, knowing the reason.

"Oh, you've got to be kidding me." He stood up. "Is Carson the smarter one out of you three? That's not saying much, considering he's not that bright."

"Come on, Nix," he said. "My parents kill me if they find out."

"They'll kill you no matter what. Then there's Grammy who'll still hurt Nathan and Carson, then there's you," Nixon told him.

"Look, we're asking you to marry us. Marrying on a ship is legal," Caleb said.

"Fine. Round up the troops. We've got a wedding to perform," Nixon said.

As Caleb and Gema were getting ready to find the others, Noah and Marcy ran up. "Nixon, we need your help," Noah said.

Nixon looked at Nash and arched an eyebrow. "Oh, let me guess. You want me to marry you?"

"Well, yeah," Noah said.

"Just because you and the other devil incarnate shared a womb doesn't mean you have to follow suit," Nixon told him.

Noah gave him an annoyed look.

"You realize that you have to face Ma and Dad along with Grammy, right?" Nash asked him.

Noah gave him a look. "Oh really, because I'm dying to see the look on their face when they find out……"

Nixon slapped his hand over Noah's mouth. "A wedding, you say. A wedding we will have. Let's go, brother dear."

Nixon escorted Noah away as Marcy asked, "What was that about?"

"Nothing," Nash said, grabbing my right hand and leading me away.

Kat and Marcy looked at each other and shrugged.

*****

We gathered as Nixon performed a double ceremony with Caleb and Gema and Noah and Marcy. That should be fun.

"Dearly beloved, I gather us here today. My brother and cousin are both dumbasses. They got their raincoats from my other stupid brother, Nathan. Is there anyone here who objects?" Nixon asked everyone as he looked around, as did we.

"No? Good. Let's continue, shall we? We know that you love and cherish each other in sickness and health, richer or poorer. Yada, yada, yada, and all that good jazz. Because we know if you don't, our fathers, along with Grammy, will beat your asses. We don't divorce," he told us.

We looked at him, then at each other.

"Let's get to the point. You love each other and want to spend your life together. When your boobs go to your knees, and you can't get it up. So, you're making the right decision," he said while the rest of us were trying not to laugh. Noah and Caleb both rolled their eyes at him while Marcy and Gema snickered.

As we stood there, a woman behind us whispered to a guy, "Why couldn't we have had him as our minister?"

The guy shrugged.

"Now, do you promise to stick it out even if one is marrying the devil, and the other is marrying the demon spawn?" He asked them.

"Do we have a choice?" Noah asked.

"Do you want me to tell Ma and Dad that you knocked up your girl?"

"Never mind."

"I thought so. Let's finish this, shall we? I now pronounce you husband and wife. Good luck," Nixon said, then walked past them.

"Well, that was a lot better than I hoped for." Marcy grinned.

Noah looked at her and rolled his eyes before kissing her, as did Caleb and Gema.

I figure they could break the news at the wedding. By then, everyone would be in a pleasant mood. At least, I hope the family is in a good mood when they find out about the double wedding on the cruise ship.

*****

After that day, the rest of the trip went well. By the time the wedding got here, everyone, except for Nixon and Kat, would be married the way they were going. They wanted a small wedding after us with family.

I couldn't blame them. Between everyone getting married and getting pregnant. Not only would we have plenty of babies, but we would start our lives as adults. It was scary but also exciting.

I was lying on the bed, thinking. Nash crawled in next to me.

"Have you ever thought about when we'd have kids, Nash?"

"Don't tell me you have baby fever." He gave me a look.

"No." I smiled. "I wondered when an agreeable time would be to start."

"Well, we could start after the wedding. Then we won't have to worry about everyone being in an uproar." Nash grinned.

"I could handle that." I smiled.

"I can't believe the demon twins got married and are having babies already. I figured they would have waited."

"Nolan will be the last to have kids."

"Are you sure?"

"Yeah, because he has three more years to go, so he'll wait. Either that or Brook will make sure of it." I smirked, causing him to chuckle.

"I can't believe in a few months that I'll dance with my wife." He held up my hand with my engagement ring and played with it.

"I can't believe that little boy next door grew up to be my soon-to-be husband." Yeah, this still surprises me.

He slid his hand into mine. "You and I forever."

"Forever."

He leaned over and kissed me.

There was no doubt in my mind that Nash would be mine forever. Everything we had endured led us to the day we would say I do. That little boy and the little girl would end up as husband and wife. Even if we didn't see it, everyone else did.

Sometimes, it takes the right people to guide you in the right direction. Those people were the Gray family.

CHAPTER 25

GRADUATION: LET THE GAMES BEGIN

After the cruise, we headed towards finishing school and graduation. Nate and Pat had everything set back home, with minor last-minute details. We would attend to them when we came home.

On a bright note, my cast came off in time for finals. I'm sure Lucille and Pat would have hurt Nash for causing me to break my wrist. Oh, I wasn't sure. I know they would have hurt him.

Everyone had to face the music when they returned home with marriages and pregnancies. It was weird to know that the devil twins will be fathers.

I wondered how Nash would be as a father. I snapped out of it as I finished up my last final. I made my way to the professor, handing him my paper, and I walked out of my final class. I was a pastry chef.

I walked out to see Nash standing there. I walked over to him.

"So, are we good?" He asked me with a smile.

I looked at him and smiled. "We're good."

He grabbed me and swung me around. Today marked the day when we finally finished school. I'm relieved. I also wasn't the only one. As each boy and girl took their last final, the ones that were graduating were ecstatic. The ones that had to remain, not so much.

The demon spawn had excellent company, with Nolan still here. God helps the school. Let's hope they don't burn it down.

*****

Graduation had arrived. It was also the day where we were rushing around like raging lunatics.

"Has anyone seen my shoe?" Noah asked while searching for his shoe.

"It's with the other one!" Nathan said.

"Or it's in your hand, you twit," Nixon said, pointing to the shoe Noah was holding.

"Oh, right," he said as he put his shoe on as he hopped down the hallway.

"Boys and girls! Get a move on, or we'll be late!" Nate said.

"We're coming! Do you have any idea how hard it is to get ready when your old lady is puking in the bathroom?" Nathan asked him.

"It's the price to pay for poking holes in your raincoat, son!" Nate told him.

"Yeah, well, I'll still kill Nathan!" Noah said.

"And thus, you don't borrow from your brother!" Nate said.

"Your mother wears combat boots!" Nathan told Noah.

"Excellent job, you tool! You made fun of your mother!" Noah said.

"Oh, appropriate point! Sorry, Ma!" Nathan told Pat.

"Nathaniel Mark Gray, Jr., I do not, nor have I ever worn combat boots!" Pat told him.

"Nashville Nathaniel! Nixon Richard! Nathaniel Mark! Noah Grayson! Nolan Daniel! Margaret Elaine, Katrina, Macey, Marcy, and Brook! We need to go!"

That was our cue as the eight of us came downstairs in our cap and gowns while Nolan and Brook followed us.

As we reached the living room, Nate and Pat looked at us. They remembered when we were little. The craziness that ensued over the years when we got older and became teens. How I came to live with them and my friends became more of a staple at their house. Now two of them are married and expecting. Another was getting ready to get married, followed by a fourth.

Nate wiped a tear from his eyes. "It's funny, I figured I would be ecstatic about this day, knowing my boys would finally be out of the house, but I'm not."

We all looked at him, surprised.

"For twenty-five years, you boys have brought your mother and me much craziness. There were also a lot of happy memories. Now, look at you, grown men, getting ready to go out on your own. I could not be prouder than I am," he said with his voice cracking.

"What your softy father is trying to say, you boys have made us so proud throughout the years. Now we're getting daughters out of it." Pat smiled.

The boys grabbed our hands and gave each of us girls a kiss on the head side.

"Come on. Let's get you eight graduated," Nate said to us. We all smiled, and as we headed out.

Jonas and Karen came to see Jace and Jaime graduate. Cayson and Dominique came after they got done yelling at Carson and Caleb. Grayson and Lucille stayed behind to deal with wedding preparations.

As they called us up to get our degrees, the Grays cheered. Our graduation relieved them. None of us were in jail, and we survived college.

I saw Frazier and his group get their degrees. I'm going to miss his crazy antics. Eh, that is okay. The Gray brothers do enough insane stuff for the Frazier's in the world.

*****

After graduation, we packed and loaded the cars, heading home. Nolan and Brook were returning next year and sharing a house with the demon spawn. Good luck, Nolan. You'll need it.

Paul had got a job offer out west, Marco and Jasper were coming back with us. Jasper would intern at the local hospital. Marco wanted to be closer to me. I couldn't blame him since I was fabulous.

I wouldn't have changed anything these past four years. Yes, they were crazy, but we survived. Now to get ready for the wedding. Why will things get crazy?

CHAPTER 26

HIS AND HER PARTY, WELL, SORT OF

We settled in at home. The boys and girls thought we needed bachelor and bachelorette parties even though we told them no. It's us telling them no, and it's the brothers listening. *Cricket, cricket.*

Yeah, that is as far as we got.

Except what I thought would happen was nothing compared to what did happen.

"Nolan, this is ridiculous," I said.

"It's genius," Nixon said.

"Aren't you supposed to be a minister?" I asked him.

"What better way than to prove my brother's faithfulness to you?" He asked as he rubbed his hands together.

"Why do I have to dress like a stripper?"

The brothers had me dress like a stripper, along with wearing a wig.

"Maggie, it's great. Think about it. Nash gets a stripper, and you don't have to worry about him doing anything wrong," Nolan said.

"Plus, we get to play one last prank on him." Nathan smirked.

"Yep," Noah said, nodding his head.

I swear these boys have no shame. I'm sorry, Nash. Please forgive me.

Nixon enlisted Kat's help. She wasn't happy about it.

"I can't believe I'm doing this," Kat said.

"You? I have to strip for my fiancé in front of his brothers and cousins," I said.

"You have a good point."

"Please tell me the girls are coming."

"As soon as we reveal you, they'll join us."

"Thank God because it sucks."

"Yep."

We walked to the door in our disguises and hooker heels. How can a person wear these shoes? I almost tripped and broke my neck about a dozen times.

We reached Nathan's house. It seemed when we returned home, Nate and Pat had secured homes for the twins. Nash and I were next in line, then Nixon and Kat, with Nolan getting one after graduating. They started the arrangements the minute we left for school.

Kat and I rang the doorbell, and Nixon answered it. "Well, hello, nurse." He winked at Kat.

"We heard someone had called for strippers," she said in a southern voice.

I stood there, speechless. Kat elbowed me. "Oh, right. We're your neighborhood strippers," I said. She gave me a skeptical look as Nixon looked at me unamused.

Nash came to the door. "What the hell?" He checked out, then said, "Nolan! I told you no strippers!"

"Nash, you can't have a bachelor party without them! It's a rule!" Nolan said to him.

"What rule?" Nash asked him.

"One that says the bachelor must get hornified!" Nolan said as the others laughed. Fantastic.

"That isn't even a word!" He told him.

"Lighten up, brother," Nathan said as he pushed him aside. "Come on, ladies. We've been waiting for you." He smirked.

We walked in with our eyes widening. It wasn't only the brothers and the cousins but also Nate, his brothers, Grayson, and their uncle Danny. Oh, God.

They dragged us in and turned on some music. Then the boys pushed Nash into a chair and shoved me towards him. Everyone walked over to us as I stood there. Kat strolled over to me. We looked at each other.

"You can start dancing any time now, ladies," Nixon spoke through gritted teeth.

We gulped and started dancing. Kat had gotten into it. I watched her, as did Nixon as he became confused.

Nash looked uncomfortable. I tapped her on the shoulder, and she winked at me, climbing off his lap. I got in front of him and started moving my body around until I slid onto his lap. "Do you like this sugar?" I asked in a fake southern accent.

"Um, well, ah," he said.

I noticed him rising to the occasion. Well, hello. He shifted in his seat as I took my tongue and licked his lips. I heard a soft moan escape his lips. Interesting.

As I continued, I almost fell with him catching me. My wig fell off my head.

"Mags?"

"Hi, sugar," I smiled.

He shook his head.

"Well, that was um, never mind," Grayson said, walking away.

Nash didn't look happy as he got up and flung me over his shoulder, carrying me upstairs. A knock came at the door, and Nixon answered it to find the girls standing there.

"Did someone mention a joint bachelor and bachelorette party?" Meg asked.

Nixon rolled his eyes as they entered the house.

*****

Nash carried me into a bedroom and closed the door. He set me down, and I said, "Before you say anything...."

He cut me off as he crashed his lips onto mine. We grabbed at each other's clothes until he had me on top of a dresser with my legs wrapped around his waist. He started thrusting inside of me as I groaned. Holy hell, this was hot. I should dress like this more often.

As he continued to thrust inside of me, we heard yelling from the other side of the door.

"Nash," I said, panting.

Thrust, thrust.

"Nash."

"Oh, God, Mags. I'm so close," he said, groaning as the door flung open.

"Can you two play hide the sausage later? We have to go!" Nixon said.

Nash stopped. "Get the hell out of here! I'm almost there!"

"I don't care if your eyes are rolling into the back of your head. Andi's water broke!"

My eyes widened as I pushed Nash away from me, leaving him with his junk hanging out.

"Mags!"

I fixed my bottoms. "Later, Andi is having a baby." I ran out of the room.

Nixon looked at Nash, then downwards. "Are you going to fix Nash, Jr.?"

Nash gave him an irritated look. "Get out!"

"I'm going. Should we have the bakers write on the cake here lies Nash, Jr.? He had a pleasant run?"

"Out!"

Nixon left, closing the door behind him.

Luckily, Macey had some clothes for Kat and me, considering we look like hookers. We arrived at the hospital except for Nash, who was dealing with a slight issue.

Jace went back with Andi as her labor continued. He was cute as a nervous wreck.

We waited in the waiting room. Twenty minutes later, Nash showed up. We watched as he strolled into the waiting room.

"Where have you been?" Nate asked him.

"Busy," Nash said.

Nate glanced at him as Nixon said, "I see you got a handle on things." He smirked.

We glimpsed at Nixon as he smirked at us. Nate rolled his eyes as I shook my head. Nash sat down next to me.

"Are you serious?" I asked him.

"No offense, but there will be no cake."

I giggled.

*****

We waited for what seemed like forever, then Jace came into the waiting room. Jonas, Karen, and Bri stood up, as did the rest of us.

"Well, Do I have a grandson or granddaughter?" Jonas asked him.

Jace smiled and said, "It's a girl!"

We cheered and hugged each other.

"How's Andi?" Bri asked him.

"She's good. Do you want to see them?" He asked her.

"Hell, yeah, I do. That's my baby sister!" She said as she hurried to see Andi. Everyone followed suit as we followed. We walked into the room and saw Andi holding their daughter.

"How is she?" Jonas asked.

"She's beautiful," Andi said, cradling her daughter.

Jace leaned over Andi and the baby. "They both are." He gave her a sweet kiss as she handed the baby to him. Watching Jace hold his daughter was amazing. You could tell he loves his daughter. God help any boy that tries to get near her.

He handed the baby to Jonas. "So, what's her name?" Jonas asked.

"What else? Lucille." Jace grinned.

"I knew my smack would knock some sense into ya," Lucille said, causing everyone to laugh.

Welcome to the Gray family, baby Lucille. Be prepared because this family is crazy.

It was a crazy night. But then again, we still had the wedding to get through. Oh, boy.

CHAPTER 27

WE INVITE YOU TO THE WEDDING OF NASHVILLE AND MARGARET

Kat was pacing back and forth as I sat on the bed, then turned to me. "You've got to be kidding me!"

I looked at Kat, not saying anything. What was there to say?

"Maggie, you only had one thing to do. You had to get your wedding dress. We got ours."

"Sorry. It's been a crazy year."

"Does anyone else know?"

"Well, no."

Kat sighed. "The wedding is tomorrow, Maggie." She sat down on my bed next to me.

"We can go to a store and buy one."

"But what about alterations? Then you'll have to make sure it's ready. People take months making sure their wedding gown is right. Everyone makes sure except for you." She gave me an annoyed look.

"I'm so dead."

"Yep, you are. Good luck with Grammy Gray."

I fell back onto the bed and sighed. Yep, good luck to me.

*****

"I knew it. I knew Mags never got her dress," Nash told Nate as they listened at the door.

"It reminds me of your mom." Nate chuckled.

"Huh?"

"Your mom forgot to get her dress until two days before our wedding. So, she left graduation with your Aunt Liz to get it. Thanks to me." He grinned.

"Wait. You bought Ma her dress."

"Yep, I talked to this lady that owned a dress shop. She had it waiting for your ma along with a note from me attached to the box."

"Well, that's great, but Grammy will kill her."

"And that's why you, my son, must always think ahead."

Nate waved Nash to follow him. They walked into Nate's room, and Pat was waiting for them.

"What's going on?" Nash asked them.

Pat looked at Nate and said, "This seems familiar."

"Yep," Nate said.

She smiled and walked to the closet, pulling out a box. She handed it to Nash.

"Here, give this to Maggie. Tell her that she owes me, grandchildren." She smiled.

Nash took the box from her. He left the bedroom and made his way to my room. Then he knocked on the door.

I opened the door. "Nash?"

"Here, Ma says you owe her grandkids," he said, holding out a white box.

I took it from him. Then he turned and walked away. I closed my door and walked over to the bed. Kat watched as I opened the box to reveal a wedding gown.

We glanced at each other. Why did it seem like Pat and Nate had been through this before?

*****

That night before the wedding, Nash stayed with Noah, as did the rest of the boys. They were getting ready together since they were standing up. The girls stayed with me, so they could help me get ready in the morning. I would need it.

I laid in bed, playing with my ring. It was weird. I would have never imagined I would walk down the aisle to Nash tomorrow. We were two neighbors that grew up next door to each other.

He would come over at night and talk to me through my bedroom window. I remembered when he started dating Sarah. My heart sank when I found out. I figured I would never have a chance. Then I ended up liking Bryson Tilson, who made my life a living nightmare.

I shook my head at that memory. I only had bits and pieces of my time with Nash before I got sick. That doctor robbed me of my memories. I could forgo the bad ones If I could keep the great ones. It didn't matter, though. My heart remembered.

My phone rang, and I answered it. "Hello?"

I wanted to catch you before you fell asleep.

"Nash." A smile curled on my lips.

It took a long time to get here, baby girl, but I'm glad we've made it. I got to thinking about everything and realized I'm so damn lucky to have you in my life. You make me a better man because of it.

My smile grew. "I never thought in a million years we would be getting married tomorrow, but I'm thrilled. Nash, you mean everything to me. It's the good and the bad. I wouldn't change it for anything. You loved me when I didn't love myself. You saw a side of me that I didn't show many people. You saw me."

Does this mean you don't have any doubts about us? Are you sure about this?

I chuckled. "That's what it means. I'll see you tomorrow."

I'll be the one standing up front, waiting for you, baby girl.

He hung up after telling me that he loved me. Then I drifted off to sleep.

*****

Nash looked at his brothers, who stood there, watching him.

"Is it weird that I'm getting married tomorrow, knowing what a complete tool I've been to her?" He asked them.

"Brother, we've always known this. It took you longer to get here," Nixon said as the others laughed.

"Nash, you have been a tool and might be a tool at various points in the future. But no matter what, you're still our brother," Noah told him.

"Yeah, you're our big brother. When you left, each of us felt a sense of loss. It was like a piece of us was missing," Nathan said.

"No matter what, you'll always be our brother like we'll be yours. We're the Gray brothers," Nolan told him.

Nash nodded in agreement. He tried not to cry, knowing his brothers would tease him since that's what they did to each other.

Nate walked over to Nash and the others. "You boys have a bond like no other. Being a brother is a different relationship than it is with most people. Your brothers are your first friends and understand you better than anyone. They have your back when life gets rough, even if they piss you off faster than anyone. You might get married and start your own families, but you'll always be brothers. Remember that."

The brothers understood what Nate said. Only they understood the bond each of them had with each other. I had been privy to see it myself. It was something I held close to my heart with them.

*****

"Maggie! What are you doing?" I heard someone asked as heels hit the floor.

"Five more minutes, Mom," I said.

"Okay, first off, I'm not your mom. She's horrible. Second, you're getting married today, you twit!" Kat told me.

I jerked up in bed. I looked at Kat wide-eyed. "I'm getting married today."

"Yes.".

"I'm marrying Nash."

"Well, that's what getting married means."

"And I'm getting married." I glanced at the clock. "In an hour! What the hell, Kat? Why didn't you wake me?" I jumped out of bed and faced planted onto the floor.

She looked at me on the floor. "I don't think a nap is a magnificent thing."

I scrambled out of the entangled blankets and ran out of the room.

"Pat! She's headed your way!" Kat said.

"I got Maggie!" Pat said.

I ran down the hallway, then into the bathroom. I showered and climbed out of the shower, drying off. The door flung open. "Ah!"

"Oh, you can relax. You have nothing that I don't have myself. Come on, sweetheart. We need to get you ready for a wedding," Pat said.

I stood there, trying to hide my naked body with a towel. I didn't have much time to wrap a towel around me when Pat grabbed me and dragged me out of the bathroom. We ran to my room, and the girls, along with Grammy, were waiting for me.

They worked on getting me ready. The girls applied my makeup while doing my hair. Once they finished, Pat held up my dress as she and Grammy helped me into it. After I was ready, I stood there as they looked at me, feeling proud that they could get me prepared.

They all smiled as I smiled back.

"Now, let's get you married," Grammy said to me as she ushered me out of the bedroom.

We walked out of my room and down the hallway. Our heels thumped against the hardwood floor as we made our way down to the main floor. They had set everything up in the backyard.

Guests had arrived and were seated. The minister was in place.

Grammy, Pat, and the girls lined up as I stood behind them. Jonas led Grammy, and Cayson led Pat. I stood there with my bouquet in my hand and my veil covering my face as I waited. Nolan escorted Brook. Next was Noah escorting Marcy, then Nathan escorted Macey. Finally, Nixon accompanied Kat.

I took my place and started to walk when someone stopped me. I turned to see Nate standing there.

"Maggie, you have always been like a daughter to me. Let me have the honor of escorting you down the aisle to my son."

I smiled. "Nate, it would honor me to have you escort me down the aisle."

He held out his arm as I took it. Then the music started. As we entered the doorway, Nash joined Nixon. He saw me and smiled. I returned the smile.

With that, Nate escorted me to Nash.

"So, does this mean I can finally call you, Dad?" I asked Nate.

"I thought you would never ask." He smiled at me.

As we reached Nash, Nate handed me off to Nash. Then Nate took a seat next to Pat. Nash and I turned to face the minister.

"Dearly beloved." *Hic.* "We are." *Hic.*

"Christ, he's as drunk as a skunk," Nixon said to Nash.

"As I was saying." *Hic.*

We stood there. Before the minister said anything else, he passed out in front of us. Everyone gasped. We stared at him, snoring on the ground.

Nate placed his head in his palm.

"Where did you find this guy?" Jonas asked Cayson.

"I got the minister out of the phone book. He was cheap," Cayson told him.

"We need to do something," Nathan said to Nixon.

"Well, I guess I can take over." He smirked.

Jace and Jaime walked towards us after Jonas talked to them. They dragged the drunken minister away as Nixon took his place. Nash leaned forward. "If you even screw this up, I'll cut off your nuts."

Nixon gave him a look. "Ye have little faith. Trust in your brother, will you?"

"This ought to be good," Nate said to Pat.

"Yep," she said.

"Dearly beloved, I gather us today to join my brother and future sister in holy matrimony. I'm going to skip the objections because we don't need them. Now, we're joining these two souls together, finally."

People nodded in agreement.

"It has been a longgggg time coming. You know, with Nash screwing up and Maggie losing her memory. But we've made it," he said with a breath of relief.

"Nix!" Nash spoke through gritted teeth.

"Oh, right. Nash, do you take Maggie to be your wife, to have and to hold, in sickness, in health, for richer, for poorer, till death do you part?"

Before Nash answered, Nixon said, "Don't answer that because you do. Trust me. We all want you to."

He turned to me. "Maggie, pain in the ass, but I love you, as in brotherly love. I don't want anyone to get any bright ideas. Do you take Nash to be your husband, to have and to hold, in sickness, in health, for richer, for poorer, until death do you part?"

Before I answered, he said, "You do. There's no way we'll give you a chance to run off now."

Nash and I looked at him.

"You shouldn't take marriage lightly. I doubt you both will do that. You can deal with Grammy," he told us as he pointed to Grammy, who nodded in agreement.

Everyone laughed.

"Anyway, yada, yada, yada, I pronounce you husband and wife. Now give her a big ole wet one," Nixon said.

Nash turned to me, raised my veil, and gave me a mind-blowing kiss.

"Okay, you can stop sucking each other's face-off," Nixon said. We stopped and turned to Nixon as he said, "I now give you Mr. and Mrs. Nashville Gray!"

Everyone cheered and whistled. Nash grabbed me, pulling me into another kiss.

"Oh, I forgot. You might want these," Nixon said as he held out his palm with our wedding rings. We took them and placed them on each other's fingers.

Now it was onto the reception. It would be one hell of a dinner.

CHAPTER 28

WELCOME MR. AND MRS. NASH GRAY

While we waited for them to clear the chairs and place the tables and chairs for the reception, we took pictures. Lucille and Grayson had one with their sons, then with the wives. Each family had a family picture taken.

The groomsmen had pictures taken with the groom, then with the bridesmaids. Then it was the bridesmaids and me. Nate and Pat took a picture with me. Then Nash and I. Lucille and Grayson had one with everyone, except for us girls. Finally, we had one large image with everyone in it.

They finally got everything set up, and we took our seats. Now was the time for the maid of honor and best man speech. Kat went first.

"I would like everyone's attention. Thank you. I have known Maggie since grade school. We have been best friends throughout these years, and let me tell you, it wasn't easy."

People laughed.

"I watched her moon over a tool when she should have been mooning over a stud like Nash."

"Kat!" Nixon said.

"Oh, hush. Your brother's hot," she said as Nixon rolled his eyes. "She also introduced me to my future husband. For that, I'll be forever grateful. To Maggie and Nash." She raised her glass.

Next was Nixon.

"Okay, my lovely fiancée gave an excellent speech, but I can top her. My twit of a brother spent years mooning over this one. Do you have any idea what it was like to hear him in his bedroom at night?"

"Nix!" Nash said.

"Dude, we know what you and Rosie were doing in there."

Nash shot him a glare. We looked at Nixon with mouths agape.

"Then Ma decided, hey, why not get them together because we know Ma is the mini version of Grammy."

Pat shrugged.

"Maggie, I'm glad you became my sister even though I used to push you down a lot as a kid. What can I say? I was an ass."

"You still are," Nathan said as everyone laughed.

Nixon rolled his eyes. "To Nash and Maggie!"

We finally got to eat. Thank God. I was starving. We ate, then it was time for our first dance. Nash led me onto the dance floor and took me in his arms. We started dancing as everyone watched.

"I love you, Wifey."

"I love you more, Hubby."

"I love the sound of that." He smiled, and I returned a giant grin. We glided all over the dance floor. It was amazing the way he held me. While we had our first dance, Pat looked at Nate. "We should have a conversation with our boys."

"You're right, Patty." He smirked.

After we finished our dance, others joined us. Then Nash and I were talking to his brothers as Nate and Pat walked up to us.

"Hey, Ma. Hey, Dad," Nash said.

"Hey, boys and daughter," Nate said to us. "It seems we have a slight matter to discuss with you."

We looked at Nate and Pat.

"So, how long did you think you could hide Nash and Maggie being already married?" Nate asked us.

"I told you they would find out," Nolan said to us. "They're better than the NSA."

"How did you know?" Noah asked.

Nate cocked his head at him. "Are you serious? The fact that Maggie didn't care what happened with the wedding preparations gave it away."

"Now, why did you keep this from us?" Pat asked us.

"Because the Gray brothers and I have been through so much together. We thought, why not do something as important as getting married," I said. "Your sons have been a huge part of my life. It was something special I wanted to share with them. I'm sorry you weren't there. Sometimes, you have to share that one special moment with the guys that mean a lot to you."

"Maggie, we aren't mad," she said to me.

"You're not?"

"No, in fact, I'm glad you could share something like this with them. You and the boys have an extraordinary bond. Even I knew that." Pat said to me, then hugged me, as did Nate.

Sometimes, you must have a special moment with the brothers.

"Okay, boys, it's time," Nate told them as they followed him to the dance floor. Pat and I followed behind them. From there, we watch the Gray boys get into formation.

Then the music started. The guys began dancing as the girls looked on. As they moved around, Nate said to Nash, "Take the lead." Nash moved to the front, and they all followed his lead. We watched as they stepped, clapped, and flipped.

I love watching them as they dance. I moved in my dress as the guys danced. It surprised the girls to watch them in action.

Next, it was the girls' turn. The Gray women moved out onto the dance floor except for Andi. The doctor hadn't cleared her yet. They started the music, and we started dancing. Pat said to me, "Maggie, take the lead." I moved to the front as we danced as the guys looked on and danced in their place.

I danced over to Nash and did a hip movement, and he leaned back. Then he followed me onto the floor, and we hopped into formation as the guys joined their women. We led them all. We had so much fun. Nash picked me up and slid me over onto his back. I landed on my feet as we came face to face.

We danced together as did everyone else. Then everyone else joined us on the dance floor. Everyone had a delightful time.

Finally, it was time to cut the cake. We picked up a piece to feed it to each other.

"How much do you want to bet they'll smash it into each other's face?" Nathan asked Noah.

"Oh, hell yeah," Noah said.

On the count of three, Nash and I smashed cake into each other's faces.

"Some things will never change with those two," Nate said to Pat.

"Nope, and I'm glad." She smiled.

Nash and I laughed, then he pulled me into a kiss. It's the little things with us.

We cleaned up and made our rounds to everyone.

"Kate? What are you doing here?" I asked Kate when we saw her.

"Maggie, you're a beautiful bride. I wouldn't miss your wedding for the world. I have a wedding gift for you and Nash," she said, handing me a manila envelope. I took it and opened it.

Inside was a blueprint of a building along with a deed.

Nashville and Margaret Gray, owners of The Gray Brother's Bakery

Nash and I stared at her with mouths agape.

"Congratulations," she said as she winked while walking away.

Nash and I looked at each other with raised brows.

"Thanks for killing my masterpiece," we heard someone say. "I worked my fingers to the bone on that cake!"

We saw Frazier and a pregnant woman.

"Oh, Hunny, get used to your cakes getting destroyed." She giggled.

"You're not helping, wife," he said.

"If it makes you feel any better, it was delicious," I told him.

He wrinkled his nose. "No, it doesn't. I'm going to find Kate." He stalked off with his wife in tow. Nash and I laughed.

We said goodbye to the brothers before leaving.

"Well, I guess this is it," Nash said to them.

"What do you mean? You're going away for a week," Nixon told him.

"Yeah, but when we get back, we're moving into our place," Nash told him.

"Oh, please, Nash. We'll end up living in different places, but we're going to be close by," Nathan said.

Nash rolled his eyes as he looked at them.

"Plus, you can't forget that Nixon is getting married when you get back," Noah told us.

"Oh, yeah," he said.

"Oh, yeah? You're my freaking best man, you twit!" Nixon said.

I couldn't help but laugh as they bickered. We might have gotten married, but I doubt we would be far from each other. Are you kidding me? These brothers will never stray far from each other.

We said our goodbyes to them, then to Nate and Pat and everyone else. Finally, we came across Grammy and Grayson.

Nash went to hug her, but she smacked him upside the head. Then she slapped me. "Ow, Grammy!" We said while rubbing our heads.

"I already took care of your brothers and cousins. Did you think you could get away with getting married before today?" She asked us with a glare.

Nash and I glanced at each other.

"Now, have fun and come back pregnant." She smirked.

Our mouths dropped open as she and Grayson walked away, laughing.

We left the reception and made our way to the limo. We climbed inside, and the driver pulled away from the reception. Nash pulled me to him and kissed me.

"I love you, Mrs. Gray."

"I love you, Mr. Gray."

With that, we were on our way to our honeymoon. I couldn't wait.

CHAPTER 29

PARADISE

We arrived at the beach house in Myrtle Beach, Virginia. Grammy gave Nash the keys to it, and we had it for seven days. We got out of the car, and Nash picked me up, carrying me over the threshold and taking me upstairs.

He carried me into a room and set me down. After kissing him, I retreated to the bathroom to change. It took time to get out of my dress. After I did, I changed into skimpy lingerie that the girls had packed for me.

I came out of the bathroom to find Nash in his boxers. I don't know why I was so nervous, considering Nash and I already had sex. Everything seemed surreal now that we didn't have to hide our marriage.

I crept over to him. He engulfed me with his arms as he captured my lips. When he pulled back, we were trying to catch our breaths. I saw the lust in his eyes, making my body heat.

Things got intense between us. He took control as his lips and hands roamed my body until the lingerie was on the floor.

"Much better. I prefer this look over the others," Nash said in a husky voice, making my cheeks heat.

Then he dropped his boxers before picking me up and carrying me to the bed. I wanted him now. My body was craving his touch, his kisses, and his whole being.

The minute he slid inside of me, I let out a groan as he started thrusting inside of me. Things got so intense that he picked up the pace until I screamed in pleasure, and he released with a loud groan.

We stopped to catch our breaths as he looked into my eyes. "God, I love you so much."

I couldn't help but smile like a fool. There's something about being with your husband that differs from a boyfriend.

"Shall we go again?"

"We can go all night long," I said, causing him to take me until we both collapsed into a peaceful slumber.

We would be spending much time in the bedroom, naked while here. That was fine with me. At least, we have privacy.

*****

I woke up the following day to find Nash's side of the bed empty and the shower running. I sat up, wiping the sleep from my eyes. A few minutes later, the shower turned off, and Nash came out wearing only a towel. He dried his hair with another towel.

"Good morning, wife," he said with a smile.

Hearing Nash call me his wife while wearing a towel with water dripping down his naked torso was turning me on.

"Morning, husband." I grinned.

He walked over to me and kissed me. Since last night was terrific, I returned the favor. I reached for his towel and pulled it from him. Then I leaned forward, placing my mouth on him.

He let out a low groan. Then I went to work, letting my tongue slide all over him, and I glanced up. He lulled his head back as he enjoyed the pleasure he was receiving. He placed his hands in my hair, guiding me.

After a few minutes, I tasted the saltiness as it invaded my mouth. Nash groaned. I swallowed and pulled away, looking up at him. His head snapped down.

"Where the hell did you learn to do that?"

"Kat gave me a few pointers." I giggled.

"Nixon is a lucky man." He smirked.

It didn't take long for him to recover as he reached down and grabbed my legs, yanking me forward as I fell backward. Then he slipped inside and went crazy.

We found our release as we groaned together. After we finished, Nash said, "We need another shower."

"Didn't you already have a shower?"

"Yeah, but I haven't with my wife yet." He smirked.

Then it hit me. Well, in that case, why not? One can never be too clean.

After we showered, we dressed and went downstairs to eat. I was starving. Nash and I made breakfast together. I could get used to this since we would work together in the bakery.

We whipped up some waffles, bacon, and eggs. Then he placed the food on the plates while I poured us some coffee. While we sat and ate, I had to ask him. "So, did you do that a lot before we got together?"

He stopped mid-bite. "Do what?"

"You know, service yourself?"

He choked on his coffee. I sat there, trying not to laugh.

He caught his breath and cleaned himself up. "Well, I didn't have many options. So, I took care of business."

I couldn't help but grin.

"What?"

"It's nothing." I shrugged.

"What, Mags?"

"It's weird to know your husband was beating off to you when you were a teen, and he was with someone else. It's cute if you ask me." I smirked.

"That isn't funny."

"It's adorable. Even back then, I could give you a hard-on." I leaned towards Nash.

"Oh, you think that's adorable?"

"Hm."

"I'll show you how adorable I can be." He gave me a seductive look, getting up and placing me on the table. Yanking aside my panties, he undid his shorts and dropped them. I don't know what has gotten into me, but I couldn't get enough of him.

As he thrust inside of me, we were getting syrup and food everywhere while knocking over our coffee. Note to self. We'll have to eat out for the duration of this trip.

After we finished, he buried his head into the crook of my neck. "Woman, what has gotten into you?"

"I can't help it, Nash. I want you all the time."

"If we keep this up, Grammy will get her to wish." He took a breath as I giggled.

He pulled out of me and pulled up his pants as I fixed myself. We showered, then we cleaned up the mess we created. Breakfast was delicious.

*****

We did leave the beach house, catching the sights and swimming. Most of the time, we were chasing each other around the house while naked. We got a little exuberant and marked every place in the house.

At one point, Nash had me bent over the counter as we went at it. Holy hell, this was insane, but I loved every minute of it. He was like a machine, and I couldn't get enough of him. I thought something was wrong with me.

In the entire time we have been together, I never once craved sex as much as I do now. Even after we eloped, I didn't want it as much as I do now. As for Nash, he was enjoying sex as much as I was.

That could be a problem.

*****

Our week ended, and we made our way home. Nash had another surprise for me. Now, what did he have planned?

It always worried me that it would be like what Nate surprised Pat with after getting married. It would be a rundown house. She told me what happened and how she had to deal with Nate and his brothers renovating the house. It's the current house they live in today.

All I wanted to do was go home and get some sleep. In a few days, we had to meet with Nate and Pat at the bakery. Kate had given them the key. It was all ready to go. They were overseeing it until we returned from our honeymoon.

We also had to get ready for Nixon and Kat's wedding. There's so much to do in such a little time. But first, I needed sleep. With that, I fell asleep with my head on Nash's shoulder. I'm exhausted but content and happy.

CHAPTER 30

WELCOME HOME, MRS. GRAY

We arrived home, and Nash parked a block away from where he was taking me. We got out of the car, and I looked around, confused. It was a street with a bunch of houses that didn't look familiar to me.

He walked over to me and swept me off my feet as he held me bridal style in his arms.

"Nash! What are you doing?" I asked with a squeal.

He looked at me with his steel-grey eyes. "I want you to close your eyes."

I cocked my head at him.

"Close them."

I sighed as I closed my eyes, then he started walking.

"Can I open my eyes now?"

"Nope, I told you, you had to wait."

I didn't know why he felt the need to carry me, but he did. Finally, he stopped and set me down. He turned me around and whispered in my ear. "Now you can open them."

I opened my eyes to see a Victorian-style house. It looked amazing. Thank God, because from what Pat told me about her home, it terrified me that I would have to go through the same thing.

Nash grabbed my hand, leading me up the pathway and onto the porch. It had a good size porch with porch chairs on it. Then he opened the door. My jaw dropped open. They had already furnished it.

"What do you think?" He asked me.

I turned to him. "It's amazing, but what about our clothes?"

"They're already in the dressers and closet. Ma and the others brought our stuff over. They also worked on the house while we were at school. It needed renovations."

"Is that why the others received houses because your parents bought fixer-uppers?"

"Ma thought Dad would hurt Jonas two hundred times." He chuckled as I giggled.

Nash closed the door and gave me a tour of the house. The dining room was to the right, and the living room was to the left. Stairs separated them. We walked through the dining room, and there was a spacious kitchen that could hold a regular size table.

Nash led me upstairs as I saw six bedrooms. The master bedroom had a bathroom. There were two other full-size bathrooms and a half bath on the main floor.

"Is there a reason we have several bedrooms?" I asked.

"Well, I always wanted a big family." He winced.

"How big are we talking?"

"Seven."

I looked at him like he lost his damn mind.

"I meant seven, including us."

"Wait. Are you telling me that you want five kids?"

"Is that a problem?"

"I don't know. Are you going to be carrying the babies?"

He arched an eyebrow. What? It was a reasonable question.

"Mags." He put his arms around my waist. "I want to have a family with you. I like big families. It's what I grew up with."

I sighed. I knew Nash loved his family. Hell, I love his family. But that is many babies. I took a deep breath and released it. "Fine, but only five. After that, you get fixed."

"Fair enough. How about we get started now?" He picked me up and carried me into the bedroom.

"Nash! We still have to meet your parents down at the Bakery, and you have to meet with Nixon!"

"They can wait!" He closed the door with his foot. From there, he gave it the good old college try.

*****

After the third time, our phones kept ringing.

"I told you we didn't have time for this." I pulled the sheet around me and answered my phone.

"Hey, we were busy getting busy." He wiggled his eyebrows as he answered his phone.

Nate told me he didn't need to hear about how we already broke in our new house. He told me to spray Nash down with the hose. I laughed. Nash told Nixon to meet us at the bakery. That way, we could kill two birds with one stone.

As soon as we hung up, Nash rolled over and pulled me to him.

"Nashville Gray!"

"Nuh-uh, Margaret Gray. I'm not done with you yet." He smirked.

"But they are waiting for us!"

"Let them wait. I need my wife to take care of my needs."

Something hard poked my buttocks. Oh, lord. We'll never leave the house.

*****

We eventually left the bedroom and the house, heading towards the bakery. I don't know if it was because we didn't have to hide our marriage, but I was frisky. What the hell is wrong with me?

I shifted in my seat. Nash glanced at me as he drove, holding the steering wheel with one hand while resting his other hand on my leg.

"Problem?" He asked.

"Ah, nope." I shifted more. Damn, I was feeling frisky.

He let out a low chuckle. "Are you sure?"

"Do you think your parents would object if we were a few minutes late?"

The car came to a screeching halt. Nash threw it into a park and released his seat belt. Then he grabbed my legs and yanked me down. "They can wait. My wife has needs that I need to take care of." I heard his zipper.

"Oh, dear."

From there, the windows steamed, and the car rocked as our moans got loud. Note to self. Car sex is exciting. What isn't exciting is someone knocking on your car window?

Nash popped his head up and hit the window button to see Nixon standing there.

"Yes?" Nash asked.

"Is there a reason your car is all steamed up and rocking?"

"Well, I'm kind of busy."

"With whom?"

My head popped up. "Me."

"I'm just checking." He smirked.

"What are you doing here?" Nash asked him.

"I was on my way to the bakery. Then I saw your car rocking with fogged windows and heard moaning. Haven't you two heard of a bedroom?"

"Brother, I don't even want to hear it from you. You might be a minister, but you also had Kat bent over the hood of your car while you pounded away."

"I've got to tell you that my fiancé is a kinky little thing." He smirked.

"I'm she told Mags that you went at it with her on the hood of your car. You're a horny little freak."

"Hey, sex is a natural and beautiful thing. So is seeing your girl's ass as you're pounding her over and over."

Oh, good, God. I didn't want to hear about Nixon's sex life. I still can't believe he's a minister.

"Well, give us a minute. We'll meet you there," Nash told him.

"Well, hurry. No one has time for you to drill your wife in the front seat of your car."

"Sorry, my wife has needs."

"Yeah, I doubt Ma and Dad will consider horniness as a need."

"Will you leave?"

"All right, finish up and meet me at the bakery."

Nixon left, and Nash rolled the window back up. He turned to me. "Now, let's finish what we started before we were so rudely interrupted."

"You don't have to tell me twice." I grinned as we went back at it. Nixon is constantly interrupting us.

*****

We entered the bakery as Nate, Pat, Nixon, and Kat stared at us.

"What?" Nash asked them.

"Do we want to know why you're late?" Nate asked.

"Nope," Nash said.

"Have you ever heard the expression if this car is a-rockin', don't come a-knockin'?" Nixon asked his dad.

Nate gave him a look.

"And a-rockin', they will be," Nixon said.

Nate rolled his eyes as Nixon smirked. After a few minutes of awkwardness, we finally discussed the wedding. They had set everything, and the ceremony would be small. This time Nate found a minister, much to Nixon's chagrin.

He wanted to perform his ceremony, but Kat put her foot down. She said anyone else's would be fine, but not theirs.

Watching them argue was like watching an old married couple. Nixon and Kat finally left as Nate and Pat stayed to talk to us.

"How was the honeymoon?" Pat asked us.

"Amazing." I sighed.

"It sounds like it." She smiled.

"Well, the bakery is all set. Here are the keys: Good luck," Nate said, handing the keys to us.

He took Pat's hand, led her out of the bakery as Nash and I looked around.

"This seems surreal." I checked out everything.

Nash walked over to me as I looked at the cases of baked goods. "Baby girl, this is our dream. One that we can nourish and grow."

I stood up straight and looked at him. "I wouldn't want it any other way." I smiled, and he pulled me into a kiss.

After Nixon's wedding, The Gray Brother's Bakery will open for business. I couldn't wait.

CHAPTER 31

NIXON AND KAT, A MARRIAGE FOR THEE

We had gotten ready and were taking our places when I needed to use the bathroom. I excused myself and made a hasty retreat. There's nothing like having to pee right before you walk down the aisle.

After I finished, my urges overcame me again. God, what was wrong with me? I heard footsteps and took my chances. I opened the door, grabbed the person, and yanked them into the bathroom.

"Mags! What are you doing?" Nash asked.

"No talking, more action." I kissed him and undid his pants. Then things got crazy in the bathroom.

"Oh, God, Nash! Harder! Faster!"

Nash thrust inside of me. I don't know what it was, but man, I was horny. I know that's crude, but I didn't care. It's like I had sex on my mind twenty-four seven. I wanted it all the time.

We finished and fixed our clothes. Then we heard the wedding march. Our eyes widened. We darted out of the bathroom, running down the hallway and the stairs.

Kat glared at us as we ran past her and down the aisle and took our places.

"Are you serious? You couldn't wait to hide the sausage later," Nixon said in a whisper.

"Dude, I don't know what has gotten into her," he said in a whisper.

"What do you mean? It's Maggie," Nixon spoke through his smile.

"Yeah, but she wants sex all the time," Nash said with a smile.

"And you're complaining?"

"No, but this is Mags. She's usually timid, but not anymore. Do you know when we went grocery shopping, she was dry humping my leg?"

"You're kidding!"

Everyone stopped and looked at Nixon. He looked at everyone. "Oh, knock it off! My brother and I are discussing that his wife was dry humping his leg."

My eyes widened, and my jaw dropped as everyone stifled a laugh. Kat was trying to be serious, but she was having a hard time keeping a straight face.

Pat glanced at Nate. "That sounds familiar, doesn't it?"

"More than you know."

*****

After the minister pronounced Nixon and Kat, husband and wife, it's our cue for the reception. I had other ideas. However, Pat stopped me.

"Maggie?"

"Yeah, Ma?" I searched for my husband.

"Is there something you want to tell me?"

"Ah, nope. I need to find Nash."

Where the hell was Nash?

"You need to do something else."

I glimpsed at Pat. What was this about now?

*****

"How is it that I get married, and your wife has to confiscate my wife?" Nixon asked Nash.

"Beats me." Nash shrugged.

"We can make an exception this one time," Nate said to them as all five boys looked at him.

Upstairs, I stood there and waited on a stick to show two lines. Pat had some suspicion when we showed up at the bakery and picked up a test.

Finally, I picked up the test and screamed.

"Can you please get Nash for me?" Pat asked Brook

"Sure," Brook said.

"Thanks, sweetheart." Pat smiled.

Brook went to find Nash. When she saw him with the boys, she explained Pat wanted to see him. They followed her back into the house and upstairs to the bathroom.

"What's going on, Ma?" Nash asked

She opened the door and shoved him inside, then closed it.

"What was that about?" Nathan asked her.

"You'll see." She smirked.

*****

I held up the pregnancy test as he crept towards me. "Is that what I think it is?"

I nodded. I couldn't even form sentences right now.

He took the test from me and looked at it.

"We're pregnant," he said.

I stared at him, then passed out.

Through the door, they heard Nash say, "Mags!"

Nate whipped open the door.

"Aww, man. Couldn't you wait until after my wedding day to put her out of her misery?" Nixon asked Nash.

Nash looked at him as Nate helped him pick me off the floor. They set me on the toilet seat as Noah picked up the pregnancy stick.

"Well, this explains it," Noah said as he passed the test around to everyone.

After everyone looked, I got my bearings.

Nash moved a strand of hair behind my ear. "It looks like we'll have to get ready for the pitter-patter of little feet sooner than expected."

"Are you sure about this?" I asked.

"Mags, I want nothing more than to have a baby with you. It might be sooner than we expected, but I'm glad." He gave me a reassuring smile.

I placed my hands on his face and kissed him.

"Yeah, yeah, it thrills us that little tools will be running around loose. Since Nathan, Noah, and Nash are having kids. Can we go back and enjoy my reception now?" Nixon asked.

"Yes, son. Stop getting your panties in a twist." Nate chuckled as he walked out of the bathroom and past Nixon.

"I'll have you know that I don't wear panties, old man!" He said as he followed Nate.

Everyone left except for Pat. I looked at her. "How did you know?"

"When I was pregnant with Nolan, I craved sex all the time. I thought your dad would lose his mind." She grinned.

Nash and I looked at each other. Oh, boy.

*****

After the reception, I was ready to go home. Nixon and Kat were on their way to their honeymoon, and I was ready for bed.

When we got home, Nash carried me upstairs.

"I would fight you, but I'm exhausted." I yawned.

"That's fine with me. Tomorrow, I'm making you a doctor's appointment. Then we have to open the bakery."

"Okay." I yawned as I drifted off to sleep.

Life was getting interesting for us. Something told me there was more to come once the bakery opened, and my pregnancy continued.

The enormous question that lingered was, what kind of pregnancy would this be, and what is the baby's sex?

CHAPTER 32

CONGRATULATIONS!

The grand opening of the bakery was in full swing, with everyone helping us. Nash called the Doctor and made an appointment for us, which was in six weeks.

Things were hectic with the craziness of the bakery. Nixon and Kat returned from their honeymoon. If I weren't tired, I would be sleeping. Did I mention other things that had popped up with the pregnancy?

I was snippy, crazy, then Zen-like, and food was delicious. I found humor in things I never thought were possible. You would think I was carrying the brothers all at once. A Gray baby came with a lot more than I expected.

Before my appointment, guess who else showed up pregnant? Yep, Kat found out she was expecting after she took a test. It was crazy with us girls pregnant. Macey was due in November, while Marcy was due in December. They're having twins. It makes sense since both are twins and married to twin brothers.

Our appointment finally arrived, and we sat in the Doctor's office. They called us back to the exam room. Nash helped me onto the table, and we waited.

A few minutes later, the Doctor came in and did his examination. It turns out I was eight weeks along. We figured it must have happened the first night of our honeymoon. When

Nash said he wanted kids, he didn't waste any time. As they say, they shoot, they score.

"Okay, let's see what's going on with your pregnancy," the Doctor said.

I laid down, and he lifted my shirt to reveal my belly. He placed this cold goop on me, then set a wand on my stomach as he moved it around.

He looked at the screen. "Interesting."

"What do you mean by interesting?" Nash asked.

"Well, I'm seeing one, two, three, and four babies." He pointed at the screen, and our jaws dropped.

"Quads?" We asked.

"It looks that way," the Doctor said as we stared at the monitor in shock.

The Doctor moved the wand around more. "Wait. One was hiding. Yep, there they are." He froze the screen.

"Quints?" We asked as we did a double-take. Who in the hell has five babies at once? We do.

"From the looks of it, I would say so," the Doctor said.

"How is that possible, Doctor? The most kids this family has ever had would be triplets," I said.

He turned off the machine and then looked at me. "My guess is you dropped three eggs. Have you had any medical issues in the past?"

"I got sick and went through an issue with the medication. The only medication I'm on now is blood pressure medication," I told the Doctor.

"Well, that could explain it. Your reproductive system could have altered. It's not uncommon for things to change when you go through an experience like that," the Doctor said.

I looked at Nash as he looked at me. "Well, you wanted your five, and now you can get fixed."

He sighed. That would teach him.

The Doctor gave us instructions. Since I was carrying multiple babies, I needed to be careful. That meant I needed to take it easy and not overdo it. That is where the family would come in handy.

*****

We left the Doctor's office, and I looked at Nash. "Five?"

"Five."

The news shocked us. It's not only that, but we had to drop this little bombshell on the family. How were we going to handle five little ones on top of running a business?

"Hey, it'll be okay," Nash told me.

"Nash, we'll need help."

"Then we'll get help. We'll have six people willing to help us." He smiled as I glimpsed at him. What did he have planned?

We gathered everyone to tell them our news. Boy, we told the family.

"Five?" Nate asked.

"Man, brother, when you shoot, you shoot. Who knew you had it in you?" Nixon smirked, earning an annoyed look from Nash.

"Okay, twins, we can understand because, well, you know we're twins and all," Nathan said. He motioned between him and Noah, along with Macey and Marcy. "Where the hell did five come from?"

"The Doctor said the medication had altered Maggie's reproductive system. They figured three eggs had dropped. It would make two sets of identical twins and one single," Nash told them.

"What will they look like?" Noah asked us.

"Well, they won't be animals. Then again, they have those two as parents," Nixon said, pointing at us. That's a reassuring thought.

Nash glanced at him. "Look, with Mags' blood pressure, it concerns the Doctor that stress could jeopardize the babies. Then we have to worry about the bakery."

"Son, what are you asking?" Nate asked.

"I'm wondering if we could get some help until the babies arrive?" He asked them. I didn't want our dream destroyed. I also didn't want to lose any of our family either. These babies were a part of Nash and me.

The boys looked at each other. With little ones on the way and Nolan going back to school, there was no way they could help us.

"How about I make a phone call?" Pat asked

"Are you suggesting what I think you're suggesting?" Nate asked her.

"Well, we know I married a smart man." She patted his cheek, then made a call.

We waited until there was a knock on the door. Nate answered it to find Jonas, Cayson, and their wives.

"Did someone call and say they needed help?" Jonas asked us.

Nate looked at his brothers. "I figure your grandbaby would tie you up and," he looked at Cayson, "isn't Caleb expecting as well?"

"Yeah, so?" Cayson shrugged.

"So, aren't you going to be busy?" Nate asked him.

"No, the boys are going back to school in the fall," he told Nate.

"Yeah, and Jace and Jaime are moving back there. Jace is moving because Andi is going to school. Jaime wants to be close to his big brother," Jonas said.

"It frees us up to help," Dominique said.

"What about Dad?" Nate asked them.

"What about him?" Jonas asked.

"Well, someone needs to watch the plant," Nate said.

"That's why you don't have any managerial skills. We talked to Dad on our way over here. He said he had someone in mind to run the place until frick and frack have their little ones," Cayson said, thumbing at us.

"Like whom?" Nate asked.

"Bucky," Cayson said.

"Bucky? That guy can't get his head out of his ass long enough to manage himself, let alone a manufacturing plant! No freaking way! I'm calling Dad!" Nate stormed off.

"That was fun," Cayson said.

"So, Bucky isn't in charge?" Nash asked him.

"Hell, no! Bucky is the last person we would put in charge. Miller runs things," Cayson said.

Nate returned a few minutes later and said, "Real cute." He rolled his eyes at Cayson as Cayson snickered.

"It's not my fault that you're gullible." Cayson shrugged.

"Okay, fine, but you have to wait on people," Nate told him.

"Fine by me." He shrugged.

We watched as they discussed who was doing what. If I even mention doing anything, I received looks. I could oversee things, but as far as doing anything, that's a big fat no.

They even enlisted my brother to help since Jasper was busy at the hospital. Why would it be pure chaos?

CHAPTER 33

BAKERY CHAOS

It had been two weeks since everyone started helping at the bakery. It's also been pure chaos. Nate and his brothers were something else with the baking. Marco was even more enjoyable.

Let's say that my brother gave a whole new meaning to flamboyant. He wouldn't stop flirting with the male customers. He was scaring the customers away and causing issues between Jasper and him. I'll get to that later.

If someone wasn't dropping something, they were burning it. It was turning into a freaking nightmare, and my blood pressure was increasing. Nash was at his wit's end, and I wanted to throw in the towel until four brothers rescued us.

They entered the bakery to see the mess.

"Damn, Daniel, what happened here?" Nixon asked Nash.

"I don't know, but it's a mess," Nash said, running his hand through his hair.

"I thought our family knew what they were doing?" Noah asked.

"No, and Mags isn't doing well. Her stress is up, and so is her blood pressure. The Doctor isn't happy," he told them.

They walked over to me as I sat at a table with my head down. I was crying. I didn't want to lose the bakery, but I also didn't want to lose my babies. My biggest fear was losing my family since I never had a proper one while growing up.

"Maggie?" I heard someone ask me.

I lifted my head and wiped tears away as I saw Nixon crouched in front of me. "Go ahead and make some stupid joke. It's not like I'm not already one." I sniffled.

Nixon pulled his brows together. "No jokes, but you need some help. It's not from them." He pointed at Nate and the others.

"I don't know what to do. You guys are busy, and I can't ask the girls to help. It's not fair to them." I sniffled.

"Maggie, we're your best friends and sisters. Family helps each other," Kat told me.

"But." I sniffled.

"No buts, you need help. We can help until Macey has the babies," Nathan said. "Then Ma and Dad can handle babysitting duties." He smirked.

"And we can help too," Marcy said.

"We can help until we return to school," Nolan said, motioning between him and Brook. Brook nodded in agreement.

"Are you sure?" I sniffled.

Nash took Nixon's place. "Yes, I called and explained to them what was happening, baby girl. They didn't hesitate to offer to help. As they said, we're family."

I nodded as Nash wrapped his arms around me, and I hugged him.

"Okay, boys, let's fix this mess," Nixon said, clapping his hands together and rubbing them together. They ousted the parents from the bakery as they cleaned up.

"Are we going to let them kick us out?" Karen asked.

"Who cares? They'll help with the bakery while we get to enjoy the babies," Pat said to her.

"Wait. We did this on purpose," Karen said.

"Have you not learned anything from Lucille?" Dominique asked her.

"Oh," Karen said when she realized what they had done.

"Come on. Let's go before the kids figure it out," Pat said as they left. The brothers also talked to Marco and straightened him out. He promised to tone it down. Well, it was that, or they would handle it. Yeah, I don't even want to know.

After they cleaned up and situated everything, Nash and Nixon made everyone food.

"Thank you for your help," I said.

"It's the least we could do with all the craziness we dragged you into," Nolan said to me.

Nash and Nixon returned with a tray of food for everyone. They put it on the table and took a seat.

"So, you never told us how the doctor's appointment went?" Nash asked Nixon.

"It went well. We're having twins," Nixon said, taking a bite out of his food.

"Twins?" We asked.

"Did I stutter? No, I didn't. What's the big deal?" He asked everyone.

"Do you realize how strange it is that we're having multiple babies at once?" Nathan asked him.

"It's not any stranger than yahoo here having five." He thumbed at Nash, who ate his food. "That reminds me. How come you have to outdo everyone?"

"How is having five babies outdoing someone?" Nash asked.

"Because you have some powerful swimmers there, buddy."

"Do you realize we'll have to buy five of everything? Then we'll have to deal with five babies, toddlers, then teens."

"You have an appropriate point. I guess your situation screws you more than the rest of us." Nixon went back to eating.

"Thanks." Nash rolled his eyes.

"So, when are you due?" I asked Kat.

"A few weeks after your due date."

I thought about it; then it hit me. "Wait. Did it happen on your wedding night?"

"The good reverend here didn't want to waste any time." She smirked.

I couldn't help but laugh. Nash and Nixon were always close while growing up. They did most things together. So, it didn't surprise me that they stayed close in adulthood.

Nixon and Kat also lived next door to us. Yep, Nixon requested to live close to Nash. The devil children were a few houses down from us, and Nolan wouldn't be far away either.

With the Gray Brothers, they were tight. Whatever they did, they did it together. I didn't mind. It would be nice to have the kids grow up together. Nolan and Brook had a few years to go.

Plus, I'm sure Nate and Pat would have fun when the grandkids arrived. They missed the boys being small. They tried to deny it, but they missed it.

After we finished eating, we headed home. The babies were giving me a run for my money.

Nash took me home, helping me upstairs. I changed, then came out of the bathroom. He was lying on the bed. He lowered a book as he looked at me.

"Your bump is the sexiest thing I have ever seen." He smiled.

"Are you sure? You don't think I look fat?" I moved my hands around my stomach.

"Fat? No, you look incredible. Come here." He motioned to me. I strolled over to him as he sat up, swinging his legs over the side of the bed. Then he pushed up my nightshirt to reveal my slight bump. He caressed it as he planted kisses over it.

"My wife is so damn sexy," he spoke in a husky voice.

The next thing I knew, he slid his hand into my panties as he rubbed me. I groaned at his touch. He applied slight pressure as I rocked with his hand.

"God, I love the way you sound." He pulled his hand away. Then he shifted out of his sweats and pulled my panties aside. I climbed on top of his lap and lowered myself on him as I straddled him. We rocked together as I moved my hips back and forth.

We didn't speak as our breathing increased until we couldn't hold back. Nash gripped my hips and thrust into me as we both released.

God, that was amazing. I wanted to sit there forever, but I knew we needed to get some sleep. Nash had other plans, as did my body as we kept going at it. I thought pregnancy makes you tired. It didn't matter since I was frisky all the time. Why would one baby be an issue when it gets older?

Which baby?

CHAPTER 34

SOMEONE GOES BUMP IN THE NIGHT

Nash and I kicked things up a notch with sex. We wanted to have some fun, so I held up a pair of fuzzy handcuffs as I sat on top of him. I dangled them on my finger.

"Don't even think about it."

"Oh, come on, Nash. I can play the cop, and you can play the sexy criminal." I jutted out my bottom lip, and he relented. I cuffed him to the bedpost. I needed to do this before he changed his mind.

As I got to work, he was enjoying himself. Boy, he loves when my mouth is on him. Then we heard a noise coming from the other side of the door. We popped our heads up.

"What was that?" He asked.

"I don't know." I shook my head.

"Give me the key."

My eyes widened.

"Mags? Give me the key."

"I don't know where the key is." I winced.

"What do you mean you don't know where the key is?"

"I sort of." I stopped before finishing my sentence. If I even finished it, it would piss off Nash.

"You sort of what?"

"Lost it." I cringed.

"What?"

I hid my face in embarrassment. We heard another thump.

"Maggie! It isn't funny!"

"I'm not laughing, Nashville!"

I got off him as he thrashed until he broke the pole in the bed frame. He got loose then fell onto the floor since his pants were halfway down.

I looked down at him on the floor.

"A little help, please," he said.

I helped him pull up his pants. He still had the cuffs on as we made our way to the living room. Then we saw a figure.

The figure kept bumping into things. "Christ! That freaking hurt!"

I flipped on a light switch to see who it was.

"Jasper?" Nash and I asked.

"Oh, hey." He waved as he fell over. We did a double-take as we looked at him on the floor.

"Mags, it seems, he's snooker," Nash said as I nodded, glancing at Jasper. Oh, boy.

*****

Nixon pushed a button on the handcuffs, releasing Nash.

"Do I even want to know how you knew how to do that?" Nash asked him.

"Did you forget who's our little brother?" Nixon asked him.

"Enough said." Nash didn't want to elaborate on Nolan's sexual hi-jinks.

"What's his deal?" Nixon asked.

They looked at Jasper as I handed Jasper a cup of coffee. I took a seat in a chair.

"Thanks," Jasper said as he took the cup and sipped the coffee.

"Jasper? Why are you here?" I asked him.

"Well, I took Marco's key and left," he said.

"Why?" Nash asked him.

"Because my boyfriend would rather have fun with other guys while I'm busting my ass at the hospital." He sighed, sipping his coffee.

"What?" I asked.

"I came home to spend time with him. With my crazy hours, I haven't seen him much. When he took a shower, his phone lit up. There were messages from another guy about how he couldn't wait to see him. He had fun the other night. That he loved his......."

"Okay, we get the point," Nixon said, interrupting Jasper.

"Do you have a problem with gay people?" Jasper asked him.

"No, I have a problem hearing anything about Marco and sex," he said.

We looked at Nixon as he shrugged. I shook my head.

"Did you ask Marco about it?" I asked.

"Yeah, he was speechless, and I left," he said as he sat back and sighed. "Do you have any idea what it's like to find out someone you love and care about is cheating on you? I can't breathe. It's like everything fell on top of me."

Jasper seemed heartbroken, and I was fuming.

Nash stood up. "We'll talk to Marco. You stay with Maggie."

"Who's this we?" Nixon asked him.

"That would be you and me, we," Nash said, with a big brother look.

"How do I get roped into these things?" Nixon asked.

"You're lucky, I guess." Nash shrugged.

"Luck has nothing to do with it. More like I'm doomed."

Nash and Nixon left the house. I stayed with Jasper as Nash and Nixon went over to Marco's house.

*****

Bam! Bam! Bam!

"Jasper! I'm so glad you," Marco said as he opened the door to see Nash and Nixon standing there. "Nash? Nixon?" He stuck his head out of the door and looked around. "What are you doing here?"

"Well, your boyfriend is at my house, interrupting my playtime with my wife. You have five-seconds to explain to me why you're cheating on him," Nash said.

"What do you mean?"

"The text messages, brainless wonder. How you and some dude had fun, and he can't wait to see you and all that other jazz," Nixon said, flailing his arm around.

"But that was a mistake!" Marco said.

"How is cheating a mistake?" Nash asked him. "Because I'm sure your sister doesn't see it that way."

"No, the messages were a mistake," he said.

"Huh?" They both asked.

"Look," he said, handing them the phone.

Nash scrolled through the message. "Christ."

"That's what I'm trying to tell you. I got a new number, and someone texts it, thinking they're texting someone else. It's a misunderstanding. I don't even know who this person is. I have the person's name in my contact list."

"So, you haven't cheated on Jasper because he's working so much."

"No, I wouldn't do that, but I didn't even have time to explain. Jasper started screaming at me like a lunatic and then left." Marco walked over to the couch and sat down. "I love Jasper. I would ask him to marry me, but he thinks I'm a cheat. I don't understand other people. How would I cheat?"

"What about the bakery? What about when you flirted with those guys?"

"What flirting? Some girls asked me to hit on them. They said it would be funny."

"Christ, this gets better and better."

"Well, we need to fix this, or I won't get any," Nixon said.

"How come?" Nash asked him.

"Because your wife will call my wife."

"Aren't you supposed to be a celibate?"

"What? No! I'm a minister, not a priest."

"And there's a difference?"

"It's a big difference."

"Can you two discuss your nonexistent sex lives later? I need to figure out how to get Jasper back," he said.

"Fine. Give me a few days. Whatever you do, don't text anyone," Nash told him.

"Okay," Marco said as Nash and Nixon left the house.

"Now what?" Nixon asked him.

"Well, now we do this the Gray way," Nash said as Nixon grinned.

This time they would need lots of help.

CHAPTER 35

FORGIVE ME

After Nash and Nixon talked to Marco, they explained to me what was going on. I wanted to be angry with Marco, but it made sense. He might be many things, but he doesn't pick up on social cues.

Jasper stayed with us for a few days. He came back after working a double one night to find Marco in our living room. He looked at him and was about to go upstairs when Marco said, "Wait."

He turned to face Marco. "What do you want, Marco? Shouldn't you be with your boyfriend?"

"But I am."

"No, your boyfriend can't wait to see you."

"But I don't understand. I explained everything to Nash and Nixon. Why are you still mad at me?"

"Do you expect me to believe your bullshit?"

"But they said they explained everything to you. Why don't you believe me?"

"Marco, the only mistake you made was getting caught."

Marco stood there with an unfocused gaze until someone walked in and said, "Are you for real? You're going to act that way."

They turned to see Paul standing there.

"What are you doing here, Paul?" Jasper asked.

"I'm here to beat some sense into you."

"Look, I'm tired, and it's been a long day." Jasper turned to go upstairs.

"Yeah, I don't care. I'm tired of traveling, but here I am."

Marco turned to Paul. "Paul, why won't he believe me? He said he loved me, but he won't believe me. What did I do wrong?"

"You did nothing wrong, Marco, and Jasper knows it. Unless Jasper has been doing things he shouldn't be."

They looked at Jasper.

"Whoa. Hold up. I'm not cheating on Marco," Jasper said.

"People accuse someone of cheating when they're cheating," Paul told him.

"Don't fucking analyze me, Paul. I'm not one of your patients."

"Then you should know Marco doesn't get the concept of cheating."

They stood there as we entered the living room. I sat down in a chair as Nash said, "Okay, enough."

The three of them looked at Nash.

"We aren't in school anymore. We're adults. Arguing over a simple text message isn't getting anyone anywhere." He looked at Jasper. "But I agree with Paul. You better come clean, Jasper."

"But I never cheated on Marco! Who the hell has time to cheat when work is so busy?"

"Then I guess we're at a stalemate."

"What?"

Nash whistled. His brothers came into the living room, grabbing Marco and Jasper. What happened next was pure gold.

****

"I can't believe this! Will you untie me?" Jasper asked.

"Nah, uh. Not until you two kiss and makeup," Nixon said.

We stood there. The brothers had tied Marco and Jasper together, facing each other. I've got to hand it to the boys. They're quick about tying up people.

"Yeah, because you two have some issues. We aren't letting you go until you resolve them," Noah said.

"But why did you tie us up?" Jasper asked them.

"We tried to do this the old fashion way, which never works," Nathan said.

"So, we did it our way," Nolan said.

"And what way is that?" He asked them with furrowed brows.

"The Gray brothers' way," they said.

"Maggie! Aren't you going to do something?" Jasper asked.

"Sorry, but I'm a Gray now. I would like to have my house back. So, you need to kiss and make up."

There's something about being a Gray that makes life more entertaining. Now I understood what Lucille meant. While most people didn't appreciate her crazy antics, I did. She wasn't stupid but fun. As a Gray, life was never dull. It wasn't always sunshine and roses, but it was never boring. She was preparing me for when I became a Gray. I needed to call her, and I did.

"Who are you calling?" Nash asked me.

"Grammy, it's been a while since I talked to her."

Hello?

"Hey, Grammy."

Maggie! How are things, my precious granddaughter?

"Oh, you know, they're good. The babies are moving like crazy."

Do you know what you're having?

"Not yet."

As I had a lovely conversation with Grammy, the boys looked at me. We talked about random things. She filled me in on what was happening with her, and I told her about the bakery.

They watched me as I had a conversation until I said, "Grammy, I'm wondering if you would help me with a little problem?"

Sure, Hunny. What do you need?

"Well, it seems Jasper won't listen to reason, so I'm wondering if you could visit and talk some sense to him?"

Their eyes widened as Jasper said, "I'll listen! *Please!*"

"I'm not sure he understands yet. Let me put you on speaker," I said as I hit the speaker button.

Jasper?

"Yes."

Don't be an idiot because you're one. That's the problem with these phones nowadays. Everyone has to text, and no one talks anymore.

"But I know what I saw."

Oh, quit your whining. You're a grown-ass man. Start acting like it. Marco might be many things, but he isn't a cheat. Although I don't understand the whole guy love thing but to each their own.

Now kiss and makeup, then leave my grandchildren's home or expect a visit from moi.

Jasper looked at us as we looked at him. Then he turned to Marco and kissed him. Their kiss was passionate, and he pulled back. "I'm sorry. Forgive me?"

"Oh, Hunny. I already did. But please don't leave me," Marco told him.

"Never."

Okay, okay, we get it. Now untie Jasper and Marco, so they can get it on at their house. I must go, but I'll be there when the babies come. Nathan, you're next. With that, she hung up.

"Great, that's what I need. Two crazy women for the price of one," Nathan said.

The brothers untied Marco and Jasper. Marco and Jasper made out in our living room as we left and turned off the lights. I didn't even want to know what they were doing. I wanted my bed.

*****

I changed and shuffled towards the bed with Nash helping me into it.

"Interestingly, you called Grammy," he said.

"Well, I figure if anyone could knock some sense into them, it's her." I grunted as I got into bed. When you have more than one baby, you get more significant than expected. The doctor was watching me and deciding when I would deliver the babies.

I laid down as Nash hovered over me. "Now we settled that issue. How about we have some fun?"

I watched as he reached under my nightshirt and slid my panties down, removing them. Then he pushed down his sweats and positioned himself between my legs. He gripped my thighs and slid into me. He thrust in and out, and we groaned as we enjoyed ourselves.

My body went crazy as he continued, leaving me in a euphoric state. Sex was amazing. Then we released, together. That was a pregnancy perk. It heightened everything.

Nash laid down next to me and pulled me close to him. His hand cradled my belly as we drifted off to sleep.

CHAPTER 36

NATHAN, MACEY, AND TWO MAKES FOUR

The months had flown by, and it was now November and Thanksgiving weekend. Nolan was home with Brook. We were getting ready for the holidays. I had gotten more prominent, so Nash and I had to get creative with sex.

The bakery was doing well. The brothers took charge. Nixon was still working with another minister, wanting to have his church one day. God, help us all when he does.

Nathan put his computer skills to work, making sure everything was online. He helped with the business aspect of the bakery while Noah managed everything. I'll admit they were incredible with these things.

Nash took care of the baking and decorating. I helped, but my movements became limited. He did most of the work. Don't worry; I compensated him at home.

Now with Thanksgiving here, we gathered for dinner. The day was going well with Macey due any day now. We didn't figure the babies would join us for dinner.

As we sat down to eat, Nixon started to say grace when Macey let out a scream. "Ah!"

"Hey, do you mind? I'm trying to say grace here," Nixon said. "Ah!"

"Are you serious?"

Nathan looked at Macey. "Mace?"

Then Macey's water broke.

"Nathan, the babies are coming!" She said as another contraction hit.

Our eyes widened as he said, "Shit!"

"Nathan language!" Pat said.

"We don't have time for that, Ma!" He stood up and helped Macey. They left the house, with us following behind them. Here we go.

*****

We waited in the waiting room while Nathan and Macey were busy delivering their twins. Nash, Nixon, and Noah were trying to make us comfortable.

I had to sit on a seat that didn't have armrests, so I could fit. It was the same thing in the car. I had to sit in the back seat. I needed more space since I'm carrying five babies.

It took a while, but Nathan appeared.

"Well?" Nate asked him.

"Do you want to meet the twins?" He asked us.

The boys helped us up, and we made our way to their room. Macey was holding one baby, and Nathan picked up the other baby.

"Meet Marshall and Murphy Gray," Nathan said.

We smiled. The babies were adorable. It made me even more excited to meet our babies. We had time to see Macey and Nathan's boys. They were a mixture of Macey and Nathan.

While seeing the twins, something felt off.

"Nash?" I said as I felt a strange pain.

"Yes, baby girl?" He asked as he turned to look at me.

"Something doesn't feel right." I winced as I put my hand on my belly.

Everyone looked at me, and he walked over. "Come on. Let's get you checked out."

He led me out of the room and helped me to find a nurse. Please, God, don't let the babies come yet. It's not time.

"God, I hope it's not the babies," Pat said.

Nate wrapped his arms around her. "I know, babe."

*****

They called my doctor, and he came in to check on me. After examining me, he decided I needed bed rest.

"This is normal for multiple babies. With five, it means things are becoming more difficult as your body is adjusting," the doctor said.

"Are the babies okay?" Nash asked him.

I looked at the doctor with equal concern.

"The babies are fine. They were moving and adjusting to the lack of room. Maggie's body is stretching. Now I want you to go home and go to bed. As of now, you're on bed rest," he told me.

As much as I hated that thought, it also relieved me. I wanted the babies to be okay.

The doctor left, and Nash helped me get dressed. Then we left the room. Anxious Grays met.

"Well," Nate asked Nash.

"I have to take Mags home. She's on bed rest for the duration of the pregnancy."

"What about the babies?" Pat asked him.

"They're fine. Mags has to rest until the babies come, which means no work and no traveling."

They looked at each other as Nash helped me to the car. It would extend the upcoming four months.

* * * * *

Once we got home, he helped me change my clothes, then helped me into bed. Great.

From there, he brought a TV inside the bedroom along with anything else. Then he left. Where did he go?

I sat there with my back against the bed frame. I rubbed my belly. "Okay, now I understand you're ready to come, but I need you to wait a few more months. Your daddy and I want to make sure you're healthy. We need you to work with us. Can you do that?"

Kick!

"Good, now you be good little ones and behave."

Kick! Kick! Kick!

"That isn't behaving." I rubbed my belly.

Thump! Thump! Thump!

"Listen, you five! Knock that shit off!"

Then there was nothing.

"Is that how I need to handle you five?"

Kick!

"Well, this is great. You're typical Gray children." I sighed.

Then I heard a chuckle. I saw Nash standing there with a plate of food.

"What's so funny?" I asked him.

"That you have to yell at our kids in utero for them to listen." He chuckled.

"I blame your genes."

"Well, I brought you food." He walked towards me.

I moved over, and he took a seat, unwrapping a plate. He handed it to me along with a fork, then picked up another plate and unwrapped it.

We dug into the food. I was hungry.

"Where did you get the food?"

"I went over to Ma and Dad's and made us two plates, then brought some extra home." He took a bite.

"What about the others?"

"I already called Ma. She said not to worry about them. You needed feeding. Plus, I'm sure they'll stop by for food."

"I love Ma." I took a bite.

"Yep, and she loves you." He smirked.

We ate, then Nash took our plates to the kitchen. He came back to find me asleep. He crawled into bed and leaned down near my belly. "Hey, it's me, Daddy. I know you five are impatient. That's the Gray gene coming out, but you must wait, okay? We want to meet you as much as you want to meet us, but we also want you to be healthy. We love you so much."

He rubbed my belly as he felt a kick, then another and another.

"Okay, settle down. Don't wake your mommy. She needs her rest. But I promise you will be here with us. You're our babies and our family. We need you as much as you need us. Plus, you're Grays. Remember that."

Kick!

Nash let out a soft chuckle as he snuggled up next to me, resting his hand on my belly. This family is what I had yearned for during my childhood. I wanted people to love and care about me. It took the neighbors to show me what a family is, even though they're crazy.

CHAPTER 37

A CHRISTMAS DELIVERY FOR NOAH AND MARCY

Since I'm on bed rest and Nathan and Macey's twins are a month old, Nash wanted to host Christmas at our house. Everyone agreed. Thank God because Christmas would suck if I had to stay in bed.

Nate helped Nash find a tree and decorate it. Pat baked and cooked food. I got stuck on the couch. Yay for bed rest. Can you tell that I'm thrilled with this arrangement?

"Oh, cheer up, baby girl. It'll be okay."

I frowned. "Nash, it's Christmas, and I can't do anything. It's ridiculous."

"Sweetheart, it's one day," Nate told me.

"Dad, you don't understand. I want to decorate the tree, bake cookies, cook dinner, and celebrate with my husband." I waved my arms around in the air.

"We know. Trust me. After the babies arrive, you'll get to celebrate with them," Nate said.

Yeah, these babies need to come soon. I was running out of the room at the inn. The doctor said each baby measured around four pounds. It's normal since multiples always measure smaller in size.

There was a knock on the door, and Pat answered it. Nixon entered with Kat shuffling behind him. She shuffled over to the couch and joined me.

"I don't know how you do it, Maggie. Two is a lot of work. But five? Good God," she said to me.

"It's because she complains a lot." Nash smirked.

I glared at Nash. "There's no fun time for you."

"Uh-huh, sure." He rolled his eyes.

"Oh, my bleeding ears," Nixon said, covering his ears.

"What are you talking about, Nixon? You're bad, too," Kat said.

"And you enjoy every minute of it," he said.

Then there was another knock. "Save by the door. Thank God," Nate said.

As Noah and Marcy entered, she shuffled over to us and sat down on the other side of me. We were a sight.

"Ugh, I'll be so happy when the babies come," Marcy said.

"Hunny, I'm trying," Noah told her.

"Well, try harder. I thought sex speeds labor up."

"Give me a break. Mr. Winky needs to recover."

"How did I get stuck in here while your mother is in the kitchen?" Nate asked with a sigh.

"I guess it's your luck." Nixon shrugged.

Then came another knock. Nate opened the door as Nathan and Macey walked in, carrying each baby.

"Pat!" Nate said.

Pat ran into the living room, knocking Nate out of the way. "Come to Nana, my precious babies," she said as she took them from Nathan and Macey. "Let's go help Nana in the kitchen." She walked off with both car seats in hand.

"So much for Ma saying hi to us," Nathan said.

"What's your problem?" Nixon asked him.

"A lack of sex is my problem. We have two more weeks to go," Macey said.

Nathan pouted.

"Dude, you don't know how hard it is not to pound the shit out of your old lady. Especially when she has a delectable ass," Nathan said.

"Have you ever heard of Rosie and lotion?" Nash asked him.

"It's not the same," Nathan said.

"Again, how did I get stuck here?" Nate asked as we heard another knock. "Thank God." He answered it. "Never mind. I'm so screwed."

"Hi to you too, Dad," Nolan said to him.

Brook saw Nathan and Macey. "Out of my way, you tool. I have babies to cuddle," she said, pushing Nolan out of the way.

"Great. Babies have superseded me," Nolan said.

"Don't worry, little brother. Your time will come," Nathan told him.

"Yeah, but it's not for a few years. Unlike you, I hid my raincoats," Nolan told Nathan.

"Why?" Nixon asked.

"Because Brook will try to poke holes in those bitches. Do you know she tried to hump me without a raincoat?"

"I can't believe any girl would want to hump you in the first place," Nixon told him.

"I'll have you know that I keep my girl satisfied." Nolan smirked.

"Whatever helps you sleep at night, brother," Nixon said with an eye roll.

Pat finished cooking dinner as Nate helped her. Nathan and Macey set the table as Nolan and Brook watched the twins. Christmas Eve was in full swing.

After dinner, we're opening gifts. We weren't expecting two surprise arrivals.

"I'm feeling wet," I said as everyone looked at me. Nash helped me up while the others checked to see why I was wet. Then we realized it wasn't me.

We turned and looked at Marcy. "My water broke," she said.

"And there goes dinner," Nixon said.

Nash went to get the others to let them know. Everyone headed out while I had to stay behind. Kat stayed with me.

"Well, I guess it's the two of us," she said.

"Is it weird that your husband left you behind while my husband left?"

The door opened. "I'm sorry, Kat. Go with Nixon," Nash said as he walked over and helped her up. She shuffled away as he sat down.

"Was it too much excitement?" I asked.

"Uh-huh. Forgive me?"

"Feed us. Then we'll talk."

He chuckled and got up, making us a plate of food.

Unbeknownst to us, Marcy had been in labor all day, so their twins came quickly. After visiting, everyone returned to the house to eat. They had left Noah and Marcy to spend time alone with their boys, Noel and Niall.

They took pictures to show us.

"You couldn't wait, could ya?" Nixon asked.

"Five babies versus a cranky uncle? Guess who wins."

He glanced at me as I smirked. Yeah, Nixon won't win this time.

During the family celebration, Nash had a special Christmas present for me.

"Come on, wife. It's time for your present," Nash said, getting up and reaching out his hand.

"But I'm comfy, Nash."

"Come on. You'll like your present." Nash and Nixon helped me up. He led me upstairs, with everyone following behind us. Pat and Macey held the twins.

Nate, Nixon, Nathan, and Nolan went to each door with Noah returning to help with my gift. Nash turned to me. "I know you thought we wouldn't be ready for the babies, but I figure this would help ease your mind. So, I enlisted some help."

I cocked my head.

"Open up the doors, everyone," Nash told them.

With that, Nate and the brothers opened a door. I walked to the first room where Nolan stood. It was a nursery. Next, it was Noah and the same thing. With each boy, I saw a nursery behind them. There were five nurseries, shocking me.

I turned to Nash. "How? I didn't even know anyone was here."

"Because we tried being quiet. Plus, it helps with noise-canceling headphones." Nash grinned.

"That's why you bought me headphones."

"With you here, how would I surprise you?" He placed his hand on my belly. Then the kicks started. I smiled at him, then walked into a nursery. I couldn't believe they set up the nurseries. I cried.

"What's wrong, baby girl?" He walked towards me.

"It's so thoughtful, and you guys are incredible. I don't know why I'm crying," I said, blubbering.

He chuckled. "Because you're hormonal right now."

I gave him a playful smack as he laughed, then he pulled me to him. Everyone else smiled at us.

The Gray family might be crazy, but there isn't anything they wouldn't do for the family. Once you became a Gray, you were a Gray.

Moving next door to them made me happy. I have sucky parents, but I received a great family out of the deal. I don't remember the last time I had spoken to my parents.

Did I need to speak to them? Nope, because I got Nate and Pat out of the deal. I received two great parents when I married their son. For that, it made me thankful.

CHAPTER 38

BABY SHOWER TIME!

We survived the holidays, heading towards the baby shower. Our doctor's visits became closer together since they needed to watch my progress. The doctor wanted to make sure we were okay.

I'm due in a month, and today is Valentine's Day, along with my baby shower. We spent the day of love doing something for the people we love, the quints.

The family had the baby shower at my house since I couldn't travel. Everyone came and helped.

Caleb and Gema had their babies. Yes, I said babies. They had triplets. Meg was expecting. Cody and Becca got engaged. Jace and Andi showed up with baby Lucille and are expecting again. Jaime and Bri got married and had one on the way. Babies were arriving in the family.

The aunts and uncles, along with Grammy and Grayson, came. Hey, when you're having five, it's a big deal.

Nash helped me dress because I was freaking huge. The babies kept growing. And well, I'm running out of room. The only problem is that my hormones were kicking into overdrive. I looked at Nash.

"Now?" He asked.

I nodded and bit my bottom lip.

"Mags, everyone is arriving, and some are already here."

"*Please,* Nash."

Boy, I needed sex right now.

He sighed. "Fine. I would usually lap this up. Since we must be quick, it's better than nothing."

I grinned, walking over to the dresser. Nash made his way over to me. He pulled up my dress and pulled down my panties. Then Nash unzipped his jeans and pushed them down. I gripped the dresser as he placed his hands on my hips then slid into me.

He started thrusting inside of me as I groaned.

"So that you know, I'm doing this because I love you."

"Cut the lovey-dovey crap and go faster, you dink!"

He picked up his pace as he pounded into me. Oh, lord. It was even better when I saw us in the mirror.

"Damn, Mags. Stop that, or you'll make me shoot quicker."

"Nash!" I couldn't even get words out as I groaned, feeling my muscles tighten and pulsate. Pleasurable waves swept over me as I kept releasing. I thought my head would explode as he thrust deep inside of me, releasing as I kept going.

I gripped ahold of him and squeezed until he had finished, releasing inside of me. He leaned over. "What was that?"

"I don't know. I couldn't stop."

"Did you have multiples?"

"I think so."

"Well, damn." He pulled out of me, grabbed a washcloth, cleaned us, and fixed our clothes.

"I like multiples." I grinned.

Afterward, we came downstairs to a room full of people staring at us.

"What?" He asked them

"You couldn't wait," Nixon said.

"My wife has needs." He shrugged.

"She has many needs," Nate said to Pat.

"Hmm," Pat said as she nodded her head.

Nash and Nate helped me to the couch as everyone talked. There were several babies, and mine were becoming a little rambunctious with everyone talking.

I rubbed my belly to soothe them. The babies were way more active than I had planned.

"Are you okay?" Nash asked me.

"The babies are active," I told him.

"I need everyone to be quiet for a minute," he told everyone.

Everyone stopped talking, then the babies stopped.

"Can I have my brothers and I speak for a minute?" Nash asked.

The boys started talking. Then it happened. The babies went crazy. I looked at Nash as he looked at me. Then something dawned on us. He had everyone be quiet again, and one by one, each of them spoke, starting with Nash.

Kick!

Next was Nixon.

Kick!

Then it was Nathan.

Kick!

Followed by Noah.

Kick!

Finally, it was Nolan.

Kick!

Nate walked over and said something, then all five kicked. He glanced at Pat. "The quints are taking after the boys."

"How is that possible?" She asked as the babies moved.

Then I looked at my stomach. "Well, okay, then." The babies moved.

"Because they feel closest to them," Jasper said.

"What do you mean?" Nash asked him.

"Because you're around them so much, they feel a connection. Babies can feel everything the mother feels. She is their direct line," Jasper said.

They all looked at me.

"Mags?"

"What can I say? You guys mean the world to me," I said, fiddling with my dress. "You gave me a family when I didn't have one. Even if you're a pain in my ass."

They gathered around me. "Maggie, you mean the world to us. We grew up with you," Noah told me.

"Yeah, you've always been a part of my life," Nolan said.

"You introduced us to our wives," Nathan said.

"And stuck by us even when others didn't," Nixon said.

Nash sat down. "And you showed us love."

"Well, you guys aren't only my brothers and husband but my best friends," I said, surprising them.

"Maggie, we didn't know that's how you felt about the boys," Nate said to me.

"Well, it's true. As crazy as things seem, you made my life better. I always wished you and Pat were my parents, and now you are. Ironic, isn't it?"

"Sweetheart, you have always been a part of our family, and you always will be," Pat said to me with a smile.

I smiled as I became wet between my legs. My eyes widened as Nash pulled his brows together.

"Mags?"

"My water broke."

Everyone stared at us with wide eyes. The babies weren't due for another month, but they had other plans. It seems the quints decided it was time to take the world by storm.

Get ready because the quints are coming. God, save us all.

CHAPTER 39

HERE COME THE QUINTS

We made our way to the hospital with the others behind us. Nash pulled up in front of the entrance and helped me out of the car. The contractions were coming quickly and painful.

He helped me inside as I screamed.

"A little help here! My wife is in labor!" He said as the hospital staff rushed to me. They sat me in the wheelchair and wheeled me back. Nash gave them my information as I screamed.

The nurse took me back as the boys ran into the hospital.

"This way!" Noah said as he ran towards the double doors.

"Sir! You can't go back there!" A nurse said, stopping them.

"Like hell, we can't! Our brother and sister are back there!" Nixon said, getting a weird look from the nurse.

The brothers pushed past her and ran to a room.

The staff had me in a bed and hooked up to monitors. "Get these babies out of me!"

"We're working on it, baby girl," Nash said.

Nixon walked over, and I grabbed ahold of his shirt.

"Get these babies out now!"

His eyes widened as my voice had gone low and unrecognizable.

"Jesus, she turned into the exorcist," Nathan said.

I released Nixon and glared at Nathan. He stepped back.

"Oh, come on, guys. Have some compassion," Noah said as he walked over to me. I grabbed hold of him and shook him as a contraction came. "A little help here!" Noah's head jerked back and forth as the brothers tried to release my death grip on him.

"Mags, let go!" Nash told me.

"I'll kill you!"

"No, you won't!"

"You did this to me! Ow!" Another contraction hit.

I released Noah, and the boys went flying backward. I screamed as they got up and scrambled around the room.

"Dude, you're getting fixed," Nixon told Nash.

"As soon as the babies come, I will," Nash said.

Everything they tried to do didn't work. A bedpan went flying past Nolan's head as he ducked. He turned and looked at me. "Why did you do that?" He asked me.

"For stealing my bras, you little asshole! Ah!"

Then I grabbed something and whipped it at Nathan, hitting him in the head. "Sonofabitch!" Nathan rubbed his head with his palm.

"That's for stealing my journal and reading it in front of the school!"

I grabbed something else and threw it at Noah, smacking him in the junk. "Holy hell!" He dropped to his knees, groaning. They watched him fall over.

"I guess he won't need to get fixed," Nixon said.

"That's for your stupid pranks!"

Then I grabbed Nixon by his crotch. "Mother of God! Let go!"

"And you! That's for being a complete douche to me!"

Nash grabbed my hand and tried to get me to release Nixon. "Mags! Let go of Nixon!"

I let go of Nixon and grabbed Nash, yanking him onto the bed. I glared at him. "Get these babies out of me, or you're next!"

His eyes widened as I shoved him away. The babies needed to come out. I was so done.

Nolan ran to get the Doctor as the doctor was on his way into my room. He ran inside and took a seat to check me.

"Doctor, please get the babies out!"

"That's what we're going to do. Because the quints are coming." He stood up and looked at me. "It looks like they're ready to make their debut. Let's have some babies, shall we?"

He made a call, and an entire staff ran to my room. The boys tried to sneak out. "*Please* don't leave me!"

They stopped and walked over to me. Nash looked at the Doctor. "Is it okay if my brothers stay?"

"If it keeps her calm, yes. But I need you to change into scrubs," the doctor said. The nurse showed them to a room and handed them scrubs. They changed.

As they headed back to the room, Nixon looked at Nash. "Let's go meet your babies, Dad."

The five of them left the room and walked down the hallway with Nash in the middle. It was a sight to see as the Gray brothers made their way to the delivery room.

They entered as Nash propped me up. My legs were in stirrups as the Doctor got ready. The brothers stood on each side of me as the Doctor said, "Maggie, I need you to push. We have five babies to deliver. Now push."

I pushed as the Doctor worked and pulled out the first baby, which was a girl. He gave me a minute, then ordered me to push as another girl came out. He cut her cord. Then once again, I had to push. Another one came, and it was a girl. He cut the cord and had me push. The fourth one arrived, and it was a girl.

I was so tired, but we needed to get the last one out. The last baby was stubborn, not wanting to come out.

The Doctor peeked around and said, "Maggie, your last one is stubborn. I need you to push."

"I can't, Doctor. I'm exhausted," I said while crying.

"Maggie, listen to us, push. Bring the last one into the world," Nixon told me.

"But I'm so tired." I didn't have it in me to deliver another one.

"*Please,* Maggie, one more push," Nathan said.

"But I can't."

"But you can. We know you. You can do this," Noah told me.

The delivery exhausted me, as Nolan said, "Come on. We'll help you." The brothers moved behind me as Nash said, "We're behind you, baby girl. You can do this. If we must hold you up, we will. Keep going. I know you're tired, but it's the last one."

I nodded as they pushed me up. I pushed, screaming, then something came out of me as I heard a cry. The last one was a boy. He cried, and I closed my eyes. Nash looked at me. "Mags! Mags! Open your eyes!"

"She's crashing! Get out of the way!" The Doctor said as the staff pushed the brothers out of the way. They worked on me then rushed me out of the room. Nash placed his hands behind his head and fell to the ground as his brothers gathered around him.

The nurses took care of the babies as the boys consoled Nash.

*****

The hospital announced a code as Jasper's pager went off. "I've got to go." He ran through the doors and made his way towards the code.

"Scrub up, Dr. Nichols," the nurse told him.

"What happened?" He asked her.

"A patient crashed in the delivery room."

He raced to change and scrub in. He held up his hands, and they placed gloves on him, then a mask. He pushed the doors open and saw me. "Maggie."

He aided the Doctor, and they hooked me up to a ventilator as they worked on me. They gave me blood transfusions as they worked to stop the bleeding.

"We have to give her a hysterectomy," the Doctor told them.

"But if you do, she won't be able to have any more kids," Jasper told him.

"If we don't, she won't live to see her children. Her family would prefer her to be here, don't you think, Doctor? Now, let's get to work," the surgeon said as Jasper nodded while assisting him.

With that, they worked on me. While I was in surgery, Nash wouldn't look at the kids as they took them to the NICU.

"Nash, you should see your kids, man," Nixon told him.

"Not without Mags," he said.

They stood there in the hallways.

"Nix, can you do me a favor?"

"Anything."

"Can you say a prayer for her? Please?"

"Sure." Nixon grabbed his brother's hands and said a prayer. "Dear Lord, please watch over our sister. Keep her safe and bring her back to us, to her babies. Lord, hear my prayers and protect her. Amen."

The brothers waited with Nash.

*****

I opened my eyes and glanced around. I was in the field. The sun was bright, and the wind blew across the grass. Then I saw someone. I walked towards the person as they turned around to face me.

"Grandpa?" I asked as I walked towards him.

"Hello, Maggie."

"But you're dead. Does this mean..."

"No, you're in surgery. There was a complication. The doctor had to take care of it. But you need to know they did it, so you can return to your family."

"I miss you, Grandpa."

"I know, sweetheart. But I know you're where you're supposed to be. Grayson fulfilled his promise to me."

"What?"

He smiled. "Let's say it wasn't a coincidence that you met the Grays and Nash."

He smiled, then walked away, disappearing into the distance.

Then I heard a voice say, "Mags. Come back to me. Please, baby girl."

With that, I turned and walked towards the voice.

CHAPTER 40

GETTING SETTLED

My eyes fluttered open as Nash leaned over me.

"Nash?"

"Hey, baby girl," he said as he stroked my hair.

"What happened

"There was a complication. For the doctor to stop the bleeding, they had to give you a hysterectomy. You can't have any more kids. I'm sorry, Hunny."

"Did we have them?"

"Who?"

"The babies."

"Yeah, all five." He smiled.

"Then, I'm good." I smiled at him as he smiled at me. "But now, I would like to see my babies."

"Good because I haven't seen them yet."

"What?"

"I was waiting for you." He smiled.

He helped me to sit up. Man, I was sore. Then he left the room. He returned with the brothers as each one pushed a bassinet. I looked at them as they stood by them. Then they pulled them from their cribs and held them up to me.

They were beautiful. I also noticed the color of the blankets. There are four girls and one boy. Oh, dear.

"So, what are their names?" Nixon asked as he held one girl.

I looked at Nash as he held our boy and said, "Meet Lyric, Larkin, Luna, Lakin, and I have Lex."

Nixon held Larkin, Nathan had Lakin, Noah had Lyric, Nolan held Luna while Nash held Lex. We wanted something different with our kids. Something told me they would be different.

Everyone else came to see the babies. I held Lyric in my arms while Nash held Larkin. The others had Luna, Lakin, and Lex.

Even though I couldn't have any more children, I was good with these five. Plus, Nash was happy he didn't have to get fixed, unlike the devil twins. They got fixed shortly after theirs, and the doctor scheduled Nixon after Kat had the twins.

"They're so tiny," Pat said, holding Luna.

"The doctor said they'll put on weight. Multiples are always tiny, but they're in good health," Nash said as he traded off with another baby. He wanted equal time with them.

"Well, I guess your mom and I can help you," Nate said, holding Lex. "Someone has to protect this boy from his sisters."

"Plus, we'll be close by," Nixon said, holding Lakin.

It would be a challenge, but we could do it. I hope we can.

After a week of being in the hospital, the doctor finally released us. Nate took two car seats since I couldn't carry anything. Nash carried two, and Pat held one.

It would be a big adjustment for us.

We came home and got settled in with the quints. Once the babies were in their cribs, we stared at them. Yes, I had the brothers move their cribs into one room. I didn't want to run back and forth. They could have their rooms when they were older.

I stood at their cribs as Nash wrapped his arms around me. "They're beautiful."

"No, they're perfect. All five babies," I said as the quints slept.

"After the doctor releases you, we're having some fun." He smirked.

I gave him a look. "It's a good thing that I bought you lotion because you have seven weeks to go, buddy." I patted his chest as I walked away. God, I was sore.

*****

It took a few weeks, but we got parenthood down to a tee.

"Throw me a diaper," Nash said to me as I tossed him a diaper and wipes.

"Throw me the powder," I said as he tossed me the powder. Then we moved to the next one. It was like a conveyor belt with the changing, feeding, bathing, and handling of the quints, but we did it. Pat and Nate helped us, so we could get some sleep. The brothers handled the bakery for us.

We also took the quints in for a checkup, and they were doing well. The quints had put on weight and were healthy, which was a relief. I was also due for my checkup in a few weeks.

Life was crazy with five little ones but so worth it. I'm used to chaos with the brothers, so parenthood was nothing new to me.

At one point, Nash and I collapsed on the bed, ready to pass out when Larkin started crying. She was our temperamental one.

Lyric is take-charge, Lakin is fussy, Luna is a little flirt, and Lex, well, he's laid back. It's a good thing because his sisters outnumbered him. It was uncanny how much they reminded me of the brothers.

We got up. Nash picked up Larkin, and she settled down.

"Geez, you would think Nixon was here." I giggled.

"Yeah, don't remind me. Kat is due next week."

"It's funny, but they remind me of you and your brothers." I picked up Lyric.

"How so?"

"Lyric is like Noah, Larkin is like Nixon, Lakin is like Nathan, Lex is like you, and Luna is like Nolan."

"Oh, God. That's a scary thought." Nash chuckled.

"But it's true. Each baby calms down when one of them comes around."

He thought about it. "That is scary."

We got the babies settled, then made our way to bed. It was exhausting but so worth it. The labor, not so much, but everything else was worth it.

We fell asleep. I knew in a few hours, someone would need changing or feeding, but a few hours was worth it. God, I miss my sleep.

CHAPTER 41

LOOK WHO'S A NEW DADDY; HERE COME NIXON AND KAT'S BABIES

Nash received a phone call in the middle of the night. "Hello?" He asked with a mumble.

Kat is in labor. We're on our way to the hospital.

"Okay." He hung up the phone.

I stirred and pushed him. "Who was that?"

"Nix."

"What did he want?"

"Kat is in labor." He fell back to sleep.

"Oh." I closed my eyes then reopened them. We got up and got dressed. We had to grab the quints. Luckily, Nathan stopped by. He walked upstairs. "Did you need a hand?"

"Yes," Nash said, as Nathan helped with Lakin. "Why are you here?"

"Nixon called. Macey told me to stop by and help you. She's staying home and getting some sleep."

"Good thinking."

We finished getting the quints ready and started downstairs when we stopped. Nash took a whiff. "Larkin? You couldn't wait." He turned around to change her.

"Damn, Larkin knows how to rile Daddy up." Nathan chuckled.

"You have no idea," I said as we continued out to the van. Yes, we were those people that needed to have a trailer to haul our team around.

Nash finally came out with Larkin and placed her car seat in its base. Then he got in and pulled out. Getting the quints ready was always crazy. Either one needed changing, one needed feeding, or one wanted to give us a hard time. Then they switched off with each other.

If I didn't know any better, I would say there was more trouble to come with them.

We pulled up to the hospital, and Nate met us outside, helping us with the babies. We walked in and set down the car seats. The babies slept while we were there. Thank God.

We waited to hear the news. I hated hospitals.

After two hours, Nixon walked out.

"Well?" Nate asked.

"Mom and sons are doing great. Kat came through like a champ. Are you ready to meet the boys?" He asked us, grinning.

"Definitely," Pat said.

We grabbed the car seats and headed back. Once inside the room, we set the quints down and saw Kat holding one baby. Nixon picked up the other one. "Meet Kaiden and Kain," Nixon said.

The twins were adorable and a mixture of Nixon and Kat. Nixon walked over, handing Kaiden to me. He squirmed, then let out a little squeak, with Lex let out a squeal.

Nash undid Lex's harness and pulled him out. He brought him close to Kaiden, and he smiled a toothless smile. Then he took him over to Kain and the same thing. I guess those three would be close.

The girls weren't having any part of it and started to get fussy. I handed Kaiden back to Nixon and picked up Luna. Nate, Pat, and Nathan picked up Lyric, Larkin, and Lakin.

It seems the girls were a little jealous of others.

*****

After visiting for a while, we headed out. I'm exhausted, and the babies needed sleep. When we got home, we put them to bed, and I crawled into bed. Nash joined me after taking care of Luna.

We laid in bed, and I cuddled next to Nash. He wrapped his arms around me, and we drifted off to sleep. I was lucky to have Nash. Not only was he a great husband but an exceptional father. I couldn't have been more fortunate than I was to have him.

*****

A few days later, Nixon and Kat brought home their boys. Everyone settled in with their families. It was crazy but worth it.

Around my eight-week checkup, the doctor cleared me. I could resume, ahem, marital duties, and we did. We had Nate and Pat keep the quints, so we could get reacquainted with each other.

It hurt like a bitch the first time, but pleasure replaced the pain after a while. Boy, we found pleasure. We found happiness in the bedroom, the shower, the living room, the kitchen, and most of the house except for the kids' rooms. Those were off-limits.

I laid on the bed while on my stomach as someone kissed my back, making their way to my neck then to my lips. Nash laid down next to me and said, "This beats lotion any day."

I giggled. "It's an excellent thing I can't have anymore, or we would be expecting another one."

"So, are you good with our five?"

"I'm more than good. Will I miss the quints as babies? Yeah, but we still have the toddler years and teen years."

"Yeah, don't remind me." He sighed.

"Is Daddy worried about his girls?"

"Nope, I'm worried about my boy. I already know my girls are bat shit crazy."

I couldn't help but laugh.

If they were anything like Lucille, I knew they were. The girls would give us a run for their money as poor Lex gets caught in the crossfire. God, save us all.

CHAPTER 42

LIFE AS PARENTS

I came down the stairs to hear Nash talking.

"Where are you going?" He asked. I watched him pick up Lakin and place her back with the others. Larkin crawled over to Lyric and climbed on top of her as he picked her up off her sister. I watched as Luna pulled herself up to a standing position at the coffee table. Lex sat there and watched them as Nash tended to the quints.

I walked over and took a seat on the floor. Lyric crawled over to me and into my lap. I situated Lyric as Nash picked up Lex, setting him on his lap while Larkin made her way over to me. Lakin made her way over to Luna as she pulled herself up to a standing position. They patted the top of the coffee table with their little hands.

"I see the kids have been keeping you busy," I said to Nash.

"I'm used to it with my brothers." He smiled as he picked up Lex and held him up. I watched as Lex giggled while Lakin touched Luna's face with her hand.

The quints were about a year old now. We would celebrate their first birthday in a few days.

There was a knock at the door as Nash stood up and carried Lex over to the door. He opened it to find Nate and Pat standing there.

"Hey, little man," Nate said. Lex buried his face into Nash since he was our shy one. Nate chuckled as they came inside. Pat tried to take Lex from Nash, but Lex refused to leave Nash. He gripped Nash's shirt as Nash reassured him.

They walked into the living room and removed their coats. They sat down, then Lakin and Luna let go of the coffee table, falling onto their butts and crawling over them. They picked up the girls and sat them on their laps.

Nash walked back over and took a seat as Lex burrowed into Nash.

"I take it Lex still has attachment issues?" Nate asked.

"Yeah, the doctor said he should grow out of it. I figure when he's an adult, he might let me go," Nash said.

Lex looked at them, then turned his face back to Nash. Nate chuckled as I held Lyric and Larkin on my lap.

"Oh, I wouldn't worry about Lex. He'll be fine. You had the same attachment issues with your dad," Pat told Nash as he gave her a look.

There was a knock on the door, and I said, "Come in!"

The door opened and in walked Nixon and Kat and their twins. Nixon dubbed them Frick and Frack. They walked over and set the boys down on the floor with the girls. We watched as Lex let go of Nash and crawled out of his lap over to the boys. It was the only time Lex didn't cling to Nash.

"Is mini-Nash still having issues with his clinginess?" Nixon asked Nash.

"The doctor said he'd be fine," Nash said.

Larkin crawled out of my lap and crawled over to Nixon. We watched as she grabbed his pant leg and pulled herself up to a standing position. He didn't hesitate to pick her up, and she cuddled into him. Nixon was the only one Larkin would cuddle besides Nash and me. Anyone else was a big no.

There were more knocks on the door as the brothers walked in with the girls and their kids. When Lyric saw Noah, she crawled out of my lap and over to him. He picked her up. Lakin wiggled to get down as Nate placed her on the floor. She crawled over to Nathan as he picked her up. The only one missing was Nolan as Luna sat on Pat's lap and pouted.

Poor Luna. Nolan was away at school and had two years to finish, along with Brook. Then we heard another knock on the door. Nash got up to answer it while the brothers played with the girls. The kids all played together while the girls and I talked.

Nash said nothing as he answered the door and waved someone inside. As Luna sat there, we watched as Nolan crept over to her. He crouched and said, "Hey, Luna Bell."

She turned her head and reached for him. He smiled and picked her up off Pat's lap.

"I thought you couldn't make it," Nate said to him.

"Our classes finished in time. There's no way I would miss my favorite quint's birthday. Isn't that right, Luna bell?" He asked her with a goofy face as she smiled big for him.

The brothers had a special bond with the quints. To see the brothers with the kids was always a unique experience. The brothers were there the day the quints were born, and the brothers would be there for years to come.

Everyone visited while the kids played. The girls were rougher as they pounced on the other kids, dragging their brother into the mix. We looked at each other as Nash placed his palm on his face. Why would we have our hands full with the girls as they age?

*****

The quint's birthday arrived. Nash made five little cakes for them and one cake for everyone else. He didn't want anyone else to make their cakes except for him. There were some things you couldn't get him to budge on, and this one of them. With the kids, Nash, along with the brothers, was ultra-protective of them.

We celebrated, then it was time for cake. Nash and the brothers placed the quints in their highchairs, then put the cakes in front of them. We sang happy birthday to them. As soon as we finished, they slammed their faces into their cakes. The quints shocked us as they demolished their cakes.

"Well, we know they take after their messy parents," Nixon said as everyone laughed. Nash and I looked at each other as the quints threw a cake at each other.

"Some things will never change," Nate said, as Pat agreed.

I couldn't help but laugh as the quint's birthday got messy. When the quints had finished, Nash and the brothers took them upstairs to hose them off and get them cleaned up. They put them all in the garden tub of our bathroom. They sprayed them down with the handheld showerhead while washing them up.

"How come your kids are the messiest out of everyone's kids?" Noah asked as he cleaned Lyric.

"Beats the hell out of me," Nash said as he cleaned Lex.

"Get back here, you little escape artist," Nathan said as Lakin crawled away, naked.

"Quit taking off your diaper, Luna. It's not ladylike," Nolan said as Luna kept trying to remove her diaper.

"Christ, Larkin!" They heard Nixon say. He carried a naked Larkin back into the bathroom while holding her away from him.

Nash cocked his head and squinted his eyes as Nixon placed her back in the tub.

"Lark decided she's an artist," Nixon said as Nash's eyes widened.

"Noah, watch, Lex," Nash told his brother as he got up and ran into Larkin's room to find her masterpiece. Yep, our child took her poop and smeared it everywhere.

I heard him call for me, and I ran upstairs. I sighed when I saw it. Nate and Pat helped us clean up Larkin's mess and sanitize her room.

With the quints, anything will happen. We were finding this out with them. There was more to come with them.

CHAPTER 43

TWO YEARS LATER: TODDLERS GALORE, ALONG WITH A WEDDING

"Lyric! You need to get ready!" I said as I walked into Lyric's bedroom.

"I don't want to get ready." Lyric crossed her arms and pouted.

"Nash!"

"Larkin, you better not take off those shoes!" Nash said. He left her room to see what was happening with Lyric and me.

"But Daddy," Larkin said.

"I mean it!" Nash said, pointing at her.

He peeked into another room. "Lakin and Luna! Stop taking your brother's clothes off!"

"But Daddy! We want to make him pretty," Lakin said, stomping.

"I said, no!" He told them as they glared at him with their steel-grey eyes.

"Fine," Luna said while crossing her arms and pouting.

Nash walked into Lyric's room. "Lyric."

"I don't want to get ready, Daddy." She jutted out her bottom lip.

He walked over and crouched in front of her. "Lyric, if you get dressed, I promise to give you ice cream at the reception."

"Do you promise?" She asked him with her big blue eyes.

"I promise," he said as he smiled at her.

"Okay, Daddy." She smiled as she got dressed.

We stood up, and I looked at him. "Ice cream?"

"It got you, didn't it?"

He pulled me into a kiss, then we heard, "Ew, yuk."

We turned to see Larkin, Lex, Lakin, and Luna standing there, sticking their tongues out at us.

"I'll ew, yuck, you," Nash said as he chased them as they squealed while running down the hallway.

I looked at Lyric. "You know you'll have to keep your sisters and brother in line, right?"

"Meh, I can do it, Mommy." She shrugged, causing me to laugh.

I held out my hand as she took it. We walked out of the room hand in hand as we made our way downstairs. We had to head over to Nate and Pat's house.

We walked in, and the kids screamed, "Nana! Grampa!"

"Come here, my favorite five!" Nate said as he engulfed them in a hug. Then we heard more screams as the kids said, "Nana! Grampa!" Marshall, Murphy, Noel, Niall, Kaiden, and Kain ran into the house.

"Oh, my boys!" Pat said as she got on her knees and engulfed them in a hug. The brothers walked in with the girls.

"Where's sex craze at?" Nixon asked everyone.

"He's upstairs, and he's nervous," Pat said.

"About what?" Nash asked.

"About Nixon performing his ceremony," Nate said.

"I'm offended. I'll have Nolan know that I have gotten better these past couple of years," Nixon said.

We looked at him.

"Yes, I have." Nixon rolled his eyes.

This wedding would be exciting.

*****

The adults had to keep a close eye on the kids. The rest of us stood up. Nixon performed the ceremony.

"Dearly beloved. We come here to join my sex craze brother and his equal sex craze girl in holy matrimony."

"What's sex craze, Nana?" Marshall asked Pat.

"It's nothing, Marshall," Pat told him, shooting Nixon a look, who shrugged.

"These two crazy kids, and I mean crazy, did what the rest of us idiots did. They're getting married."

"What's an idiot, Grampa?" Noel asked Nate.

"Your uncle Nixon," Nate told Noel.

"Now, we know, you say I do because, well, if you didn't, we've wasted our time," Nixon said.

"Daddy's crazy," Kaiden said to Kain.

"Uh-huh. Mommy said he pounds well. I'm wondering if he pounds blocks," Kain said as Kaiden shrugged.

"Now, we'll cut to the chase. You love each other. Because if you didn't, well, we would have a serious issue."

"Is Uncle Nixon weird?" Niall asked Murphy.

"I don't know. Daddy said he lost his marbles." Murphy shrugged.

"I got marbles if he needs them," Niall said.

"Uncle Nix is a big fruit loop," Larkin said.

"I like Fruit Loops," Luna said.

"Fruit Loops are awesome," Lakin said.

"Shh, Daddy will get mad if you keep talking," Lyric told them, putting her finger to her lips.

As Nixon kept talking, we heard Lex ask, "Daddy, will you be mad if we keep talking?"

We stopped as Nash placed his face in his palm. "No, buddy, but can you be quiet?"

"Uncle Nixon, I have marbles for you. Daddy said you lost yours!" Murphy said.

"No, I got marbles! Uncle Nixon, you can have mine!" Niall said.

Nate and Pat were trying to stifle their laughter.

"I want Fruit Loops, Daddy!" Luna said.

"Yeah, can we have Fruit Loops, Daddy?" Lakin asked.

"Hey, can you get your kids under control, so I can finish this ceremony?" Nixon asked us.

"Daddy, do you pound blocks with Mommy?" Kaiden asked.

We looked at Nixon, trying not to laugh.

"You were saying, brother," Nash said as Nixon rolled his eyes.

"I now pronounce you, man and wife. Kiss your bride. I have to take care of a kid," Nixon said as he walked off the stage with Kat following him.

"Kaiden and Kain!" Nixon said as he stormed towards his twins.

"Nash," I said, giving Nash a look.

"Right," Nash said, running after Nixon.

While Nash handled Nixon, the rest of us dealt with our kids. After Nash calmed Nixon down, Larkin ran up to him. She wrapped her arms around his legs. "Uncle Nix!" She squealed.

"Hey, girlfriend," he said, picking her up.

Lakin ran over to Nathan, and he swooped her up. Luna ran to Nolan, who did the same as Lyric yanked on Noah's pant leg. Lex went over to Nash and reached up.

"Up," Lex said to Nash as Nash picked him up.

The other boys played together as I looked at the boys with the quints.

"You know, it's weird they have a bond with them," Marcy said.

"I don't think so," I said.

"What do you mean?" Macey asked.

"Nash and I figured it out. The quints are like the boys with their personalities. They have a bond to each brother," I said.

The girls looked at the brothers as the boys talked to each quint.

"Well, all I can say is good luck, Maggie. If the quints are like the brothers, you'll need it." Kat smirked.

I placed my palm on my face.

The reception started, and Nash made sure the quints had ice cream. We ate a scoop of ice cream together. Lyric and Larkin had Nash's hair color and my blue eyes. Lakin and Luna had my hair color and Nash's steel-gray eyes. But Lex was Nash's mini version since their resemblance was uncanny.

As we sat there, a little girl shuffled over to the table. She must be the quintet's age. She tugged on my skirt, and I looked down. "Hi, would you like some ice cream?"

She nodded with big brown eyes.

I lifted her, placing her on my lap. I let her have my ice cream and looked at her. She had brown curly hair and brown eyes. Then I looked at Lex, gazing at her.

"Piper!" We heard someone say from a distance.

She turned her head as a man walked over to her. "There you are, sweetheart. You worried your mom and me."

She reached for the guy, and he picked her up.

"Piper!" A woman ran up. "Oh, thank God! We're so sorry. We were unloading our car and noticed she had wandered off," the woman said.

"It's not a problem," I told them.

"We're sorry," the man said.

"It's fine," Nash said. "Did you say you were unloading?"

"Yeah, we moved in a few houses down. There's a family next door with five kids," he told us.

"You don't say," Nash said.

"We're glad because we were afraid there wouldn't be any kids in the neighborhood," the woman said to us.

"Well, I'm Maggie Gray. This is my husband, Nash Gray. These are our quints, Lyric, Larkin, Lakin, Luna, and Lex," I said, introducing my family.

"I'm Mike, and this is my wife, Nancy. This little wanderer here is Piper," he said, tickling Piper as she giggled.

We invited them to join us, and they did. It was weird. I figured history would repeat itself, but Mike and Nancy were nothing like my parents. I was glad because no kid deserves to have people treat them the way my parents had treated me. It worked out for the best.

CHAPTER 44

THREE YEARS LATER: OH, GOOD GOD

I was bringing clothes upstairs. I stopped as my eyes widened, dropping my clothes basket.

"Nash!"

"What?"

"Can you come to Larkin's room?"

"Yeah!"

I heard his footsteps coming down the hallway.

I stood there, stunned. Nash walked up and stopped. "You have got to be kidding me." He walked into the room and over to the quints. "Girls, how many times do I have to tell you to stop dressing your brother in dresses?"

"But, Dad, he's a pretty girl," Lakin told him.

"He's not a doll," Nash said as he picked up Lex and hauled him out of the room. He stopped and looked at me. "Can you talk to your daughters? I have to save our boy." He walked away, holding Lex like a football. Lex waved.

I walked in and crossed my arms as I looked at the girls.

"Girls, what have we told you about dressing up your brother like a girl?" I asked them.

"Not to do it when Dad is home," Larkin said.

"And?"

"If we make him pretty to make sure we use colors that bring out his coloring," Luna said.

"And?"

"If Dad is home, and he catches us, you're the bad guy," Lyric said.

"Right, because Daddy will have Mommy's head," I told them. They smiled as I turned to see Nash leaning next to the doorframe with his arms crossed.

He motioned to me with his finger. I walked over, and he said, "Lyric, you're in charge. Mommy needs a spanking." He pointed out of the door.

"Ooh, mommy is in trouble," Lakin said.

*****

We turned on loud music as Nash gave me my spanking. Boy, he spanked me on the bed, on the dresser, in the bathroom.

We finally collapsed onto the bed.

"I love my punishments." I grinned.

"I bet you do." He chuckled. Then he turned to me. "Mags, please stop encouraging the girls to put Lex in a dress."

"Well, I didn't get to do it with your brothers."

"It's our kids, not my tool of brothers."

"Oh, fine. I promise not to let the girls dress him in dresses anymore." I sighed.

Then we heard, "Uncle Nix!"

Well, shit. We scrambled off the bed as we got dressed and left the bedroom.

Kaiden, Kain, and Lex ran past us to Lex's room. We came downstairs.

"So, the girls were telling me mommy got a spanking." Nixon smirked.

"Only because mommy is allowing the girls to dress my boy in dresses," Nash said, glancing at me. I shrugged. Then there was a knock. I answered it, and Piper ran over to the girls. They ran upstairs as Nancy and Mike came in.

"Hi, Piper!" I spoke.

"Hi, Maggie!" She spoke.

"She kept begging to come over." Nancy chuckled.

"She's more than welcome to come over anytime," I said.

We talked as the demon spawn arrived with the girls, along with the boys.

"When's chow?" Nixon asked.

"As soon as Nolan and Brook get here with the boys, along with Ma and Dad," Nash said. Then Nolan and Brook showed up with their three-year-old twin boys, Brody and Beau, with Nate and Pat following them.

"Now we can eat," Nash said as he walked over to the twins, who were gripping Nolan's legs.

"Do you boys want to play with the others?" He asked them.

They buried their heads into Nolan's pant legs.

"Marshal! Murphy!" Nathan said.

"Yeah, Dad," Marshall said.

"Come get Beau and Brody," he told them.

"Sure thing, Dad," Murphy said.

They walked over to the boys. "Come on, guys, we'll protect you," Murphy told them.

"But they're mean," Brody said.

"Not with us around," Marshall told them.

"I don't like them," Beau said.

"Aw, they're pussycats," Murphy said to them.

"Daddy, please don't make us go," Beau told Nolan.

Nolan crouched and looked at them. "How about if Uncle Nash talks to them?"

They clung to Nolan.

Nash turned and said, "Lyric, Larkin, Lex, Lakin, and Luna, get your butts down here!"

The quints came running downstairs and over to Nash.

"Yeah, Dad," Lyric said.

"I'm warning you five. If you touch one hair on Beau and Brody's head, you won't sit for a month," he told them.

"It's not our fault they're wimps," Larkin said.

"Larkin," Nixon said with a look.

"Fine," she said, crossing her arms.

"They're big babies," Lakin said.

The brothers, including Nash, gathered and faced off with the quints. They were the only ones that could go head-to-head with our five hellions. They had the same personality.

"Listen up and listen well. There will be no shenanigans from you five, or you'll deal with the Gray Brothers," Nathan said to them.

They stepped back as the brothers stepped forward.

"Or we'll deal with you the Gray way. Capeesh?" Noah asked them.

The quints nodded.

"So, if you're thinking about it, we've already done it," Nolan said.

"Because we are the Gray brothers," the brothers said.

With that, the quints ran off.

"I knew our shenanigans would come in handy," Nash said to his brothers.

"Don't they always?" Nixon asked.

Beau and Brody followed Marshall and Murphy to play with the others as the adults talked.

Who knew moving next to troublemaking brothers would end up like this? I didn't, but I'm so glad I did.

CHAPTER 45

SAYING GOODBYE TO A BELOVED FAMILY MEMBER

The quints had turned twelve and were even crazier. A preteen meant their hormones were in overdrive, getting ready to hit puberty. We dealt with their craziness. The brothers dealt with their kids' pubescent craziness.

Amid everything, Nate and Pat received a phone call from Grammy Gray with news about Grayson. It wasn't good.

Nate went to the airport with his brothers to gather their mom and Grayson's casket. They had flown Grayson back to Michigan to bury him in his family plot. The funeral director took his body straight to the funeral home as the boys took Grammy to Nate's place. The funeral would be in a few days.

Everyone came to pay their respect to Grammy, and it was hard on everyone. Grayson seemed like a gruff man, but Lucille and his love had been one in a million. She dealt with it the best way she knew how her way.

*****

We got ready to head to the funeral home. Nash warned the quints not to start their shit. Yeah, they had a habit of doing things inappropriate in these situations.

We arrived at the funeral home and greeted everyone. I walked over to the casket and saw Grayson looking peaceful. Others joined me. Then I heard someone say, "Yep, he had a wonderful run." We turned to see Grammy standing there.

"Did you need anything, Lucille?" Pat asked Grammy.

"Patty, what I need is lying in that casket. Other than that, I'm good, Hun."

"I'm sorry, Grammy. I liked Grayson," I said.

She smiled at me. "And Gray liked you. He was very fond of you, dear."

I smiled. I had gotten to know Grayson on vacation after high school. He was a serious man at first. Afterward, he had lightened up and was funny.

Nate walked over to us. "Do you need anything, Ma?"

"Nope, I'm good, unlike your father, who went out with a colossal bang," she said.

Nate groaned, turned, and hurried away from his mother and over to his brothers.

"What's wrong with you?" Cayson asked Nate.

"Ma is telling everyone how Dad died during sex," he said.

"Ew, gross," Jonas and Cayson said.

"She's something else," Jonas said while shaking his head.

We paid our respects as everyone greeted each other. It had been a while since I had seen the cousins. They had changed somewhat, and their kids had grown. I also had to wrangle the quints before they burned down the funeral home. Nash and the brothers shot them a look, making them settle down.

Everyone took a seat, and Nixon went up front to offer a prayer along with a few words, then Lucille wanted to speak. We watched as Nate and his brothers placed their palms on their faces. It's never good if Lucille was speaking.

She stood up and walked to the front. She glanced at Grayson and then turned to face us.

"So, as you know, Gray is no longer with us. He had a pleasant run, and he had filled his last moments with happiness. He's a Gray, and Gray men are virile men," she told everyone.

We sat there speechless as Nate and his brothers groaned.

"Gray was special to me and needed to loosen up. After he did, he had a lot more fun." She grinned a toothy grin as I sat there, realizing this would be an exciting funeral.

"No one knew that Gray had his moments when he wasn't a jackass. Like most couples, we had our difficulties, but we still loved each other. He had a temper. Lord knows his anger got him into trouble, but he also had a good heart. When he became a father, he was ecstatic, even if he had to take the boys in hand most of the time. No one knew he had gotten a tattoo of a tree with a family saying while on our honeymoon. I asked him about it. He said family keeps us rooted when we need it. He believed the family was important, and I do, too. Family matters and is everything. Always remember that." She walked back to her seat.

I looked at Nash as he looked at me, then we looked at the quints. I knew what Lucille meant. Even if the quints were crazy, they're still our babies.

*****

We attended the funeral and watched Lucille place her hand on Grayson's casket, then lean down and kiss it. It was her last goodbye to him until she left us to join him. Let's hope that's not for a while.

After the funeral, we went back to Nate and Pat's house to eat. People always make a lot of food, even though you don't feel like eating. Grief sucks and kills your appetite.

Nate and his brothers decided that Lucille was moving from Florida to Michigan. She sold her house in Florida. The boys didn't want their mom to live alone. Now, that's fine and all. When deciding who she'll live with, Nate had the pleasure. Jonas and Cayson volunteered him. I thought Nate would hurt them.

I can see it now. Life would get more interesting with Lucille living with Nate and Pat. We also had the brothers and their families close by us. Sometimes, we need a reminder of our roots and who we are. I learned from the Gray family that family is everything and has a bond like no other. I'm glad that I had sucky parents because I got a great family in their place. Thanks to the Grays, I met my future husband and the father of my kids.

My parents are rotting in jail somewhere. Eh, it serves them right.

CHAPTER 46

HERE COMES THE GRAY SISTERS

"Ma! Larkin is a pain in the ass again!" I heard Lyric say.

What are they doing now? There's always something going on with Lyric and Larkin.

"Tell Luna to put on some clothes, Ma! Her ass is hanging out again!" Lakin said.

"Only because I have an ass unlike you!" Luna said.

"Christ, must you idiots argue?" Lex asked them.

"Who asked you?" Larkin asked.

Is it sad that I must hide from my children in my bedroom closet? Dealing with five crazy seventeen-year-olds was ridiculous.

"What the hell is going on here? You knock it off! Luna, change your outfit! Don't give me that look! Lakin, stop your bitching. Lex, go find something productive to do with your life!" I heard Nash tell them. Thank God he was home.

The door opened and closed, then the closet door opened. I glanced at Nash. "Hi, Hunny." I gave him a slight smile.

"Are you hiding again?"

I nodded. "When does school start?"

"In a month." He chuckled, holding out his hand as I took it. He helped me up, and I kissed him.

"I can't wait to get back to the bakery." I sighed.

"I know, baby girl."

"Ma and Dad called. They want us to come over and see Grammy."

"This ought to go over well with the hellions." He sighed.

"Yeah, well, Grammy can handle them." I smirked.

"I can't believe it's been five years." He sighed as he hugged me.

"I know, Hun." I hugged him back.

Crash! Break!

"Now what?" Nash looked at me as we left the bedroom. We came downstairs to see the front window broken with glass scattered on the floor.

"What the hell happened here?" Nash asked.

"They did it." The quints pointed at each other.

"That's it! I've had enough of your shit! Starting tomorrow, you'll work at the bakery to pay for this damn window!" Nash told them as he got met by resistance from the quints.

"But I have a date," Luna said.

"And I have plans with Jessica," Lakin said.

"I'm busy," Larkin said.

"I have plans with Piper," Lyric said.

"Do you?" Lex asked her.

"Yeah, I do. Why?" She asked him while giving him a strange look.

"There's no reason." He shrugged.

Nash scowled at them. "Cancel them. You're working. Do I need to call your uncles?"

"No, no," they said.

"Then get your shit together, or your senior year will be a long year," he said. "Now clean up this damn mess. I'm taking your ma out."

"What about us?" Lakin asked.

"You should have thought about that before you broke the living room window. Oh, and I want it boarded up. Lyric, you can call Uncle Cayson and explain why we need a new living room window," he told them.

Nash took my hand and led me out of the living room. We got into the car, heading out to dinner.

Life was better when they were little. The minute they became teens, they turned into little hellions. I miss them being little.

Life would get crazier, and their senior year would start it all. If you thought the Gray Brothers were crazy, you haven't seen anything yet with the Gray sisters.

Poor Lex. He would get caught in the crossfire of what would happen. God, helps us all.

To continue in The Gray Sisters.

Printed in Great Britain
by Amazon